CAN YOU SURVIVE 2020

An Interactive Adventure

by

Andy P. Smith

Design by Adam Bezer
Illustrations by Fahri Muaffa

Also by Andy P. Smith

100 Things Phish Fans Should Know & Do Before They Die

Welcome to the Land of Cannibalistic Horses

In a year fraught with distress, pain, and sorrow,
I aim to offer humor and entertainment.

This book is dedicated to you.

You are a young writer and working bartender in South Williamsburg, Brooklyn. You've been living in New York City for almost 10 years after moving to the city for college. You're from Portland, Oregon and you visit your parents there often.

Today is March 6, 2020.

The Coronavirus is plaguing Europe and it now seems that New York City may be a new epicenter of this growing pandemic.

What's worse is that you just got laid off, via text message no less. The owner of the bar you work at sent a group message to you and the other bartenders saying he had no choice but to close the bar and is making his decision now so you can apply for unemployment as soon as possible.

Maybe now you'll finally have time to write?

This whole thing will probably blow over by Memorial Day anyway.

At home, in your tiny studio apartment, you go online to complete the Department of Labor application for unemployment. Then, you start pricing flights to Portland. You've been thinking of taking a trip and visiting your parents. Now, without a job, it seems like the perfect time.

There's worse places than Portland to spend a few weeks. And flights are pretty cheap. But you love New York. This is where you live! It does feel a bit like running away but maybe Portland will be a bit safer from the virus?

Should you stay or should you go now?

Book a flight to Portland, turn to page 2.
Stay in New York City, turn to page 5.

Hell, why not go to Portland? See your parents, get some fresh air. You could use a break from the city. And if the Coronavirus continues to spread in New York City, it's probably better to be in Portland anyway.

You buy your plane ticket for the next morning with a return ticket for two weeks later. You clean out the refrigerator and make yourself a smorgasbord for dinner. You call your parents and let them know. They're thrilled you'll be visiting.

"Do you have a mask you can wear on the flight?" Your dad asks. Both of your parents are retired nurses.

"Really?" you ask.

"Can't hurt," your dad says. "We'll pick you up at the airport."

You say goodbye and dig out a small bag of tools in your closet from when you and your friends sanded down the fireplace mantel and painted your bedroom. Sure enough, there's a pair of contractor dust masks. You toss them into your backpack and start pulling out clothes for the trip. You fit everything you think you'll need for the next two weeks in your small suitcase.

Feeling good, prepared, you make one last round in your studio to make sure everything is ok for you to be away: you water your one half-dead plant, lock the windows, and stand in the kitchen looking around... for some reason you get a strange feeling you may never see this place again.

You shake it off, brush your teeth and get into bed with your laptop. You put on "Tiger King." It's truly stranger than fiction, you think, smiling. And you fall asleep to the piercing yet somehow comforting voice of Joe Exotic.

In the morning you call a Lyft and get to the airport with plenty of time before your flight. Good thing too! The airport is crowded and everyone is stressed. More than a few people are wearing masks. You hear your dad again, saying, "Can't hurt." You put on your mask too.

The flight is long and uncomfortable. Every cough or throat clearing you hear makes you more and more worried and stressed. What if you get Coronavirus on this flight? And then infect your parents? Or worse, what if you already have it? What if you infect people on the flight?

You text your dad through the flight's wifi: "I'll take a cab home, don't worry about picking me up."

He pushes back a bit, says your mother will be disappointed but he'll see you soon. The chat proceeds:

You: Does your neighbor still have that RV?

Dad: Yes, George?

You: Do you think he'd let me crash there for my visit?

Dad: In the RV???

You: Yeah. Can you ask him?

Dad: Why not stay in your old room in the house?

You: Just thinking about social distancing. Will you ask him?

Dad: It'll break your mom's heart if you don't stay in the house.

You: Can you ask?

Dad: Yeah I'll ask.

Your flight lands and you can't get out of the airport fast enough. You get a Lyft and even through your mask now feels kind of gross and annoying, you don't take it off.

You: In a car, see you soon!

Dad: Great!

You: Did you ask George?

Dad: You can stay in the RV

Relieved, you let your head fall back against the headrest of the carseat. It's the first time you've relaxed even a little bit since you left your apartment for the airport.

Maybe you're overreacting. You don't have Coronavirus. But damn, what if you did? And then your parents get sick. It seems that younger people don't have serious symptoms but older people do. There were all those terrible deaths in that nursing home in Seattle.

Better safe than sorry, for sure. But it would break your mom's heart if you didn't stay in the house and be close. You can still hang outside, your parents have a beautiful deck with a BBQ and a large backyard. It wouldn't be so bad, the weather isn't so bad. Staying in the RV could be kind of fun. It's not like you wouldn't be able to hang out.

Play it safe, right? Or maybe you're overreacting?

In a perfect world, you'd stay comfortably in the house. But this is far from a perfect world.

You feel fine, though. Mayebe this is just a scenario of perceived risk versus real risk in which there's actually no risk at all.

Hell, this whole thing could be some weird hoax. What if it's just 5G-related radiation or something?

Then again, what if it's the real thing?

You're almost at your parents house and probably best to make a decision before you arrive.

Quarantine for two weeks and stay in the RV, turn to page 7.
Stay in the house, it's not a big deal, turn to page 13.

Yeah, New York is home, you're not going anywhere. It'll be good, some down time, time to focus on yourself, do some writing.

In just a week, New York City completely shuts down. It's scary, like a ghost town. Stores even boarded up windows. No one on the streets. And come nightfall, the streets around your apartment, once comfortable and welcoming, now feel very ominous and dreadful. Then it gets worse.

You hear ambulance sirens every day, and night too. And at 7pm most days you join the rest of the neighborhood – the whole city, really! – and lean out your window to clap or bang on a pot to support and champion the front line workers at the hospitals that are now installing refrigerated shipping containers on the street as make-shift morgues.

They build a field hospital in Central Park, a sight you'll never forget.

You drink, heavily. You're not getting much writing done, but checking in with friends on Zoom and watching at least one movie every night.

March becomes April and nothing much changes. Except now you can hear birds? Just one day, you started hearing birds. At first you think it's someone's phone alarm or something, but no. You hear genuine bird song coming from outside your apartment. No people, no cars, no honking, or anything… just birds. And you weep, uncontrollably.

The next week you start to exercise, going on runs and doing YouTube workouts. Then you start baking, which you'd done before but never really took to it. You decide you're going to start painting and order a watercolor set online.

On Monday evenings you watch a livestream of Reverend Vince Anderson performing in his living room. On Fridays you watch the livestream archive shows from The Grateful Dead while doodling. Most other days you facetime your friends who live outside of NYC, and some of the ones who do live in NYC.

Suddenly, it's Memorial Day Weekend and things are starting to look up. The weather has improved and so has your mood, if just a little bit.

Your friend Jimmy, a fellow bartender, invites you to join

him at an afternoon rooftop BBQ, which he claims will be very chill and socially distant with all the right amount of safety and precautions. But still, you're skeptical.

How could anyone honestly host a socially distant BBQ?

Then again, it would be really nice to see other people and hang out and pretend like everything is safe and normal

Maybe it's worth going to the BBQ?

Maybe so, maybe not?

Go to the BBQ, turn to page 11.
Stay home where it's safe, turn to page 15.

You arrive at your parents' house and grab your suitcase from the trunk of the Lyft. Your parents' house looks really nice, comforting. You can see your neighbor's large RV parked on the side of the house.

Your mom, likely waiting by the window looking for your arrival, comes out of the house with a big smile. Your dad follows slowly behind her.

"I'm so glad to see you!" your mom says, stretching out her open arms. "You're going to stay in the house, right?"

"Mom, I think I should stay in the RV," you say. "And we should maintain social distance, which sadly means no hugs. I'm sorry, it's just the smart thing to do."

"Ok," she says. "I don't like it, but I understand. We'll grill outside for dinner?"

"That sounds great," you say, a bit teary-eyed.

"Glad you're here," your dad says.

"Are you hungry?" your mom asks. "Thirsty?"

"Yeah, I could have a drink," you say, laughing through your tears.

"Why don't you get settled and meet us on the back deck?" your mom says.

"The RV is unlocked," your dad says.

"Great," you say, "That sounds great, thanks."

You take your suitcase into the RV. It's bigger than you expected, and kind of cool. It's a bit musty, and you open some windows. This is going to be fun, you think.

Soon you meet your parents on the back deck. They've put a chair and a small table with a glass of wine and a plate of cheese and crackers on the opposite side of the deck from where your mom is sitting and your dad is working the grill.

"I also have some potatoes in the oven," your mom says. "Baked potatoes with everything on it, your favorite!"

"That sounds wonderful," you say. "Baked potato with all the fixings."

A nice breeze blows through the trees. It feels good to be home.

Time passes and most days are the same: hanging out on the back deck, reading, talking with your parents, texting and calling old friends, eating, drinking, it's easy and comfortable.

As the days become weeks, you cancel your return flight. New York City seems increasingly dangerous. Besides, your new RV home is about the same size as your Brooklyn apartment.

After a few weeks, you move out of your neighbor's RV and into your parents' house, sleeping in your old room, using a real shower, and sneaking midnight snacks when you can't sleep. There's still a sense of doom underneath all the childhood comforts, but most days you feel alright.

April turns to May, and suddenly it's Memorial Day. At first you thought this would all blow over by now, but it seems like you may never return to New York. You're receiving unemployment and still paying rent on your Brooklyn apartment, which seems kind of silly, but you're actually earning more on unemployment than you did bartending.

You wake up on Tuesday, May 26th, 2020 and read in the news that the police have killed another unarmed black man. This time, it's in Minnesota. His name was George Floyd. A grocery store clerk called the police after Floyd allegedly bought a pack of cigarettes with a counterfeit bill. The cops arrived, moved quickly to violently arrest him, and choked him to death on the sidewalk while he begged and pleaded that he couldn't breathe.

You're upset and angry and sad and it feels like there's nothing you can do to change anything.

The virus, police brutality, unemployment, climate change, wealth inequality, the upcoming election… it all hits you like a ton of bricks, like a bucket of water, like a sledgehammer to the chest.

You decide to get involved. Over the next few days, you find some local activist groups online, add a schedule of protests to your calendar, and take some YouTube lessons on deescalation and protest tactics. You've never felt so impassioned in your life.

Your neighbor loans you a bicycle and you ride to downtown Portland to participate in a scheduled Black Lives Matter protest march. Arriving downtown, you lock up your bicycle and join a small group of people walking towards where you believe the larger group is marching.

The sun is shining and you feel powerful in the crowd. Everyone wears a mask and many are carrying cardboard signs calling for justice for George Floyd and Breonna Taylor. Other signs read Black Lives Matter and some read Defund the Police. One organizer uses a megaphone to lead a call and response from the crowd. "Whose streets?" she says. "Our streets!" you chant with the rest of the crowd.

Your group converges with another group and grows larger. It feels fantastic to be out, amongst it, so to speak. After months at your parents house just waiting for something to change, you finally feel some sense of purpose.

For now, there seems to be no real police presence as the crowd continues marching. You pass a pair of people handing out supplies from a parked van to protestors passing by: bags of chips and bottles of water. It's now mid-afternoon and getting hot. You're thirsty so you take a bottle of water.

"Thank you," you say.

"Here take two," the aid says, handing you another.

You decide to take a moment and sit on the curb to drink some water before continuing the march. You estimate you're a few miles away from where you parked your bike. You take off your mask to drink some water.

Suddenly, a fellow protestor sits down on the curb next to you. "It's getting hot," she says, from behind her black bandana.

"Sure is," you say.

"Nice to take a break," she says.

You hand her your extra bottle of water and she thanks you before removing her bandana to drink it. "You going all the way to City Hall?" she asks.

"I suppose so," you say. "I'm just kind of going with the flow here." You notice she has a phone number written in sharpie on her arm.

"It's important that we get numbers at City Hall this evening," she says. "But Friday is the big rally."

"What's happening on Friday?"

She looks you up and down as if she's trying to determine if she should trust you.

"I want to help," you say.

"If you're serious," she says. "If you truly want to support change and justice and you're ready to fight for what's right, then meet me at the 5th Avenue Cinema tomorrow night at six."

She puts her bandana back on and stands up to rejoin the march.

"Wait," you say. "What's your name? Maybe we should exchange numbers? I'm not sure I can make it tomorrow but--"

"Leave your phone at home," she says, and disappears into the crowd.

A bit bewildered, now realizing how tired and dehydrated you really are, you decide to leave the march, make your way to where you parked your bicycle, and ride back to your parents' house.

You eat leftovers for dinner and skip the family movie to read up on uprisings and dissent throughout history. You also look up the 5th Avenue Cinema and discover it's a small one-screen cinema run by students and all screenings are free to Portland State University students.

Eventually, you go to sleep and have weird nightmares about martial law and police brutality.

The next day you once again ride your bike to downtown and join a demonstration. This time, you've packed a bag of food and water and sunscreen and even a change of socks. It's a long day but you feel great. So far everything has been peaceful but you're not sure if it's really going to effect change.

It's almost 5:30pm now and you've made your way back to where you parked your bike, not far from the 5th Avenue Cinema. You're intrigued by the invitation but also who was that girl and why would she invite you? Maybe it's worth checking out, you can always leave. Then again, maybe it's something in which you really shouldn't get involved.

Check out the 5th Avenue Cinema, turn to page 16.
Call it a day and head home, turn to page 21.

Screw it, you're going. You'll be cautious, wear your mask the whole time, and keep your distance. Not sure how you're gonna drink a beer with your mask on but you'll figure it out.

You make your way to the BBQ address and Jimmy is there waiting for you outside. "Hot damn," he says. "Here you are!"

"Here I am," you say.

"Come on, let's head up," Jimmy says.

The building's door is propped open and you both take the stairs up and up and up to the roof where, surprise, it's packed with people. The music is loud, everyone is talking closely, most have masks but many do not. This isn't exactly what you had hoped for, you're pretty anxious about the scene, but you're here so you roll with it for now.

You have a few drinks and your anxiety dies down. It's actually really nice to be outside among people. Your friend Jimmy is hilarious and it feels so damn good to laugh with others. You meet some new people, which feels strangely unfamiliar but all good.

One of the new people you meet is this very talkative woman named Quinn. She's blonde and bubbly, and has a lot of opinions, namely that COVID-19 is a manufactured virus, a biological weapon. "It's true," she says. "My boyfriend is a pharmacist and he's collecting the evidence we need to break open this whole thing and expose everyone!"

"Uh-huh," your friend Jimmy says.

"Your boyfriend is a pharmacist?" you ask.

"Or a biologist?" she says. "He works with diseases and medicines. They actually asked him to work on COVID and he said no."

"Who asked him exactly?" Jimmy says.

"The Chinese," Quinn says.

"Right," Jimmy says and gives you an eye roll.

"People think that they're in control," Quinn says. "Everyone thinks that what they see is real."

Jimmy just looks at you. But you're intrigued.

"What do you mean though?" you ask.

"Like," Quinn says. "Like, there's a whole plan for the

planet and it's run by this one group of people and no one even knows it."

"The deep state?" you ask.

"What's that?" Quinn asks.

You can't help but laugh.

There's just something about Quinn.

"My boyfriend is so much better at explaining these things," she says. "You guys should come over and meet him. He's probably done working for the day. We have some weed, do you smoke?"

"Everyone smokes weed," Jimmy says.

"Not everyone!" Quinn argues. "But yeah, I should've brought some. Let's go to my place and smoke, ya wanna?"

"I'm gonna stay here for a bit longer," Jimmy says.

"Ok," Quinn says. "What about you?"

Go meet the boyfriend, turn to page 18.
Pass on the invitation, turn to page 24.

You arrive at your parents' house and grab your suitcase from the trunk of the Lyft. Your parents' house looks really nice, comforting. You can see your neighbor's large RV parked on the side of the house.

Your mom, likely waiting by the window looking for your arrival, comes out of the house with a big smile. Your dad follows slowly behind her.

"I'm so glad to see you!" your mom says, stretching out her open arms. "You're going to stay in the house, right?"

"Yes, mom," you say, embracing her in the driveway. You hug and it feels great, you've made the right decision. You hug your dad and the three of you head inside the house.

Immediately, your mom hands you a glass of wine and a snack plate. The house is immaculately clean and your parents are just beaming with happiness. This is the life, you think.

You enjoy a nice, healthy, home-cooked dinner before everyone settles into the big comfy couch to watch the new Jumanji movie. Everything is right.

The next few days are completely relaxing. You don't have a care in the world. Your friends in New York City text you about how weird it is there during lockdown and you can't help but feel good about your decision to leave.

As the days go on, you settle into a nice pattern of home-cooked meals and PG movies.

Then, one morning, your dad wakes up with a gross, terrible cough. He says he feels ok, but the next day your mom says her stomach has been bothering her. And you can't help but think she looks a bit pale.

It's been over a week since you've been home and you haven't really been worried but now you're concerned. You dig out a thermometer from the bathroom medicine cabinet and convince your parents to take their temperature.

First your dad: 101°. Then, after cleaning the thermometer with rubbing alcohol, you take your mom's temperature: 102°. And then, after another cleaning, you take your own temperature: 98°.

You panic. They both have fevers and other Coronavirus symptoms. They calm you down and convince you it's probably just a summer cold.

But a few days later, they're not any better.

Then, in the middle of the night, a commotion wakes you up. You get out of bed and make your way to the kitchen where you find your parents. Your dad looks terrible and is having trouble breathing. You can see the fear in your mom's eyes.

"I'm taking your father to the hospital," she says.

"I'm coming too!" you say.

"No," she says, coughing. "You stay here and I'll call you shortly."

But she didn't call. And she's not answering her phone. You take a Lyft to the hospital where the admin says that both your parents have been intubated. Your father is very sick and is in a medically-induced coma. They won't let you see them.

Two days later, your father dies. And the next day, you convince them to let you see your mother. She can't speak but you can tell she knows you're there. Gently, she passes.

You're now an orphan. Perhaps if you had quarantined when you arrived, your parents would still be alive.

For the time being, you've survived 2020.

But the insufferable guilt of infecting your parents will stay with you for the rest of your life.

THE END

It's Memorial Day Weekend but that doesn't mean you can party safely. You can't drink with a mask on anyway. But at home, you can do whatever you want!

You decide to cook an early dinner, veggie fajitas, and put on Remain in Light by Talking Heads really, really loud. You're happy, at least for a moment, chopping peppers and onions, listening to one of your favorite bands.

You open a can of black beans, put some rice on, and think, yeah, let's smoke a little pot. You dig out a bag of weed, untouched for weeks, and put a small nugget into your pipe and smoke it. Exhaling a large, white cloud of smoke, you smile. Quarantine isn't so bad!

You finish cooking and enjoy your vegetable fajitas with a nice bottle of wine. It's now dark and you take a glass of wine to bed with you and prop up your laptop to watch "Tiger King." It's been out since March but you missed the initial buzz and then kind of forgot about it until now.

A little stoned, a little drunk, a belly full of fajitas, you drift off to sleep in the glow of your laptop and the soothing sounds of Joe Exotic discussing his love for tiger cubs.

You dream you're watching a band perform in a zoo? Then, you awake in your bed, but pretty out of it. The laptop is off and from outside your apartment you can hear music, a DJ. You roll out of bed and look out the window to discover a large, full-on block party. Everyone has masks on, having a good time, dancing to the music.

You check your phone: it's 10:30pm, you slept for a couple of hours, and now you don't know what to do. You're not going to go back down easily, especially with this party outside. Hell, maybe you should go down and check it out. Keep your mask on, and see what's what. If you can't beat 'em, join 'em, right? Then again, you do have seven and a half episodes of "Tiger King" left to watch. These are the tough decisions of our time.

Stay in and binge Tiger King, turn to page 27.
Check out the block party, turn to page 33.

You ride your bike to the cinema and at first just slowly cruise past, scoping it out. The cinema has been closed for months and it doesn't look like anything is going on inside and no one is hanging around outside. You park your bike about a block away.

Walking up to the building, you can't help but feel like you're being watched. But the few people on the street all seem disinterested in you. You approach the three glass doors of the cinema. Looking in, the place seems empty. You gently try to pull the door and it opens.

Without thinking you duck inside and close the door behind you. The daylight through the glass doors gives enough light to see the concessions counter and the door to the theater and the place seems completely empty and still. You think to call out but remain quiet as you make your way to the theater.

Suddenly the theater door opens and two people dressed all in black are coming towards you. "Did you bring your phone?" one asks as the other one moves past you towards the door.

"No," you say. "I was told not to bring my phone."

The person behind you locks the glass doors to the cinema. "Good," she says.

It's the girl who invited you.

"I'm glad you came," she says. "This way." And she and the other person lead you into the theater.

It's a small room, less than 100 seats, and there's maybe 20 people in there. Everyone is dressed in black and most are wearing health masks. Everyone seems very serious.

"Go ahead and take a seat," she tells you as she walks to the front of the theater. She then speaks to the group, saying, "We all know why we're here."

Except that you don't really know why you're there. But soon, it all becomes very clear. This is a militant group of activists. And it seems that they've been planning a series of coordinated actions. Suddenly, you're fearful of being here. Maybe you should leave.

You stand up and head to the door but the leader, the woman who invited you, calls out your name. You turn to face her. You never told her your name.

"We're all very grateful to have you here with us," she says. "We're proud of you. We're all in this together, together we can make real change. We can show them that we're not going to allow our country to fall to Fascists and authoritative regimes. We will not tolerate living in a police state! We're here to do something about it! Dammit, we must do something about it!"

You stand there with everyone in the room looking at you.

"We need you," someone says.

"We need you," another person says.

"We need you," say two others in unison.

"We truly, truly need you," says the leader. "You're not here by accident. We've been waiting for an opportunity like this. Please, stay."

It all feels like a movie. And you still have no idea what they're even talking about. And how did she know your name?

They're all watching you.

What will you do?

Get the hell out of there, turn to page 22
Hear what their plan is, turn to page 25.

"Ok, yeah, sure," you say. "Let's go."

Jimmy just groans.

"Great!" Quinn says. "I'm not far from here, we can walk!"

So you and your new friend Quinn leave the rooftop BBQ and head towards her apartment. She continues to talk during the walk moving quickly from one topic to another: climate change, incarcerated Chinese muslims, ICE, SpaceX, Malaysia Airlines Flight 370… it's weird but fun. Something different at least!

"This is it!" she says as you come upon a beautiful West Village townhouse. "We can hang in the garden."

You enter the home, what should be or likely once was a multi-family house, and you're blown away by the grandeur and decor of the space. Quinn takes you through the main entryway and living room with huge windows and natural light, through the spacious kitchen with spotless stainless steel appliances, and out an open sliding glass door to an open, lush garden that's bigger than your entire apartment.

Sitting in a large rattan chair is a handsome man with long blonde hair and a blonde beard reading a book. The whole scene, particularly his linen outfit and bare feet, makes it seem like you're no longer in New York City but rather some bizarro paradise free of COVID and all of your anxieties.

"Honey, I'm home!" sings Quinn skipping towards him.

He looks up from his book and smiles, standing to greet her. Quinn's diminutive stature makes him look like a giant but even without the comparison he is very tall, looking something like a viking. They hug and kiss passionately.

"I made a new friend," Quinn says to him and then introduces you.

"My name is Jonas," he says. "It's just so dreadful that we cannot shake hands these days." He pulls a cotton mask from his shirt pocket and puts it on. "Can I offer you a drink?"

"Oh, no thanks," you say, still reeling a bit from the beauty and opulence of everything, not to mention the truly bizarre pairing of these two as a couple.

"I said you'd explain the whole thing about Corona," Quinn says as she bounces back into the house.

Jonas laughs a bit. "Well," he says. "I don't know if I can

explain the whole thing but we can certainly discuss it, yes."

You take a seat in one of the rattan chairs and relish in the scene and your decision to join. You could hang out here often.

Quinn comes skipping back outside with a bottle of champagne and glasses. Handing one to Jonas and one to you, she then pops the champagne.

Sure, ok, you think. Why not?

While enjoying the champagne in the late afternoon sun in this beautiful garden, you listen to Jonas tell you this rather insane story. He begins by explaining his background, that he's a biologist and virologist from Sweden and was involved with the UN and peacekeeping missions and worked as a consultant evaluating war crimes and chemical warfare... Saddam Hussein attacking Iran, the Bosnian War, Syria... not knowing much about the history of these wars and countries, it's hard for you to fact check him but also the relaxed nonchalant tone with which he tells these stories gives you no doubt of his honesty.

Then things get weird.

One day Jonas finds himself in a meeting, "sitting among the deep state," he says, he realizes he's now included in the inner sanctum. "And the scope of the conversations that happened in those meetings was truly global and... interstellar."

Quinn hums the theme song to "The X-Files."

"But none of that really bothered me," Jonas says. "What bothered me was discovering that we are currently in another Cold War, this one with biological weapons. These scientists, these virologists, have developed diseases so intricate and so precise that many of them, if released in large populaces, would be more deadly than a nuclear attack. Do you know how many people died when the US dropped nuclear bombs on Japan?"

You shake your head.

"199,000 souls were lost in Hiroshima and Nagasaki, Jonas says. "And while incomprehensibly tragic, not to mention the suffering that followed. Well, with COVID-19, we're now approaching 100,000 deaths just in the United States. And over five million have been infected worldwide."

Suddenly the champagne you're drinking tastes bitter.

Quinn chimes in, saying, "But we're going to expose them for the assholes they really are!"

"Expose who?" you ask.

"Whom," Jonas says, correcting you. "We're going to expose the true leaders of the world, the puppet masters who work in the shadows, for who they really are: murderers. This disease, this COVID-19, it didn't come from bat soup, do you really believe that?"

"I guess not," you say.

"This is a biological weapon," Jonas says. "This is malice and greed and a secret war that will cost the world millions of innocent lives. Now, not everyone wants to believe this, not everyone wants to hear this, and if you'd rather not learn more about this, that's totally acceptable. We can discuss something else."

"What do you mean?" you ask.

"It's like when you go see a fortune teller," Quinn says. "And she asks you if you want to know the day you're going to die. They don't just blurt it out and tell you. You have to make the choice to learn certain things, stuff you can't ever unlearn, ya know?"

"Ok," you say. "Yeah, I'm not sureI want to know the day I'm going to die?"

"No, silly," Quinn says. "It's only *like* that, we have no idea when you're going to die."

"Would you like to discuss further?" Jonas asks.

You take the last sip of your champagne. This whole thing took an unexpected turn. It's been weird and getting weirder. But where are you going to go? Back home to sit by yourself? Or maybe get a little drunk with these weirdos and hear what else they have to say?

"I'll open another bottle!" Quinn says, jumping up and skipping into the house.

Leave and go home, turn to page 32.
Stay and listen, turn to page 37.

With COVID there's enough reason to exercise caution and prudence. Marching in an outdoor protest is one thing, but meeting up with random stranger indoors at a cinema is another level.

You bike home.

Continue, turn to page 23.

This all feels just a bit too much.

And without hesitation, you turn heel, run back to your bike, and pedal all the way home without looking back.

Continue, turn to page 23.

You walk into your parents' house and find them cleaning the kitchen and washing dishes after dinner. You're sweaty and panting and still a bit weirded out, but seeing them in their routine is comforting.

"Oh, honey," your mom says. "You got a letter."

"A letter?"

"Yeah, in the mail," she says. "It's on the counter there."

On the counter next to the junk mail catalogues is a plain white envelope with your name and address on it. But something's not quite right about it. Also, who would be sending you letters to your parents house?

"This came in the mail?" you ask.

"Uh-huh," your mom says at the sink washing dishes.

You're still trying to figure out what's strange about it and then suddenly it hits you: there's a stamp but it's not postmarked. Did someone personally deliver this letter and leave it in the mailbox?

"Thanks," you say. "I'm going to take a shower."

You hustle into the bathroom, turn the shower on, and stand there with the letter.

Is this from the protestors? Or someone in the neighborhood maybe?

The mirror begins to fog from the steam of the shower as you look over the envelope for clues. There's nothing beyond your name and address written neatly in pen on the envelope.

Part of you says you should just throw it away.

But of course another part of you wants to open it.

Rip it up and throw it away, turn to page 30.

Open the envelope, turn to page 36.

"Another time?" you say.

"Yeah, fine, ok, whatever," Quinn says. "It's always the same with people like you."

"People like who?" Jimmy says.

"People who act like they're non-judgmental and free spirits and open to new people and new ideas," Quinn says. "But when it comes down to it you're just shallow, scared, cliquey people like all the 'boomers' you make fun of."

"Whoa," you say. "There's no need for that. We just met and our friends are here so we're going to stay, ok?"

"My momma raised me right," Quinn says. "I was always taught that if someone invited you somewhere, you accepted the invitation. But I guess some people weren't raised right."

"I'm done with this," Jimmy says, pulling on your arm. "Come get another drink with me."

"No, wait," you say, then turn to Quinn. "You don't know me. You don't know anything about me, how I was raised, what I'm scared of, or what I really want."

"Yeah?" Quinn says. "You really want to stay here and piss the night away when you could do something new, try something different? If that's true, then fine. But if not, you owe it to yourself to get out of your comfort zone and see what this stranger is really talking about."

The three of you stand there in silence for a moment as the wind blows through Quinn's hair.

What the hell, go meet the boyfriend, turn to page 18.
Stay at the party, who cares she says, turn to page 28.

"Ok," you say. "I'm listening."

"Our plan is simple," the leader says. "We're here to cause non-violent disruption of the police state and prison industrial complex."

Everyone is watching you for a reaction.

"What does this have to do with me?" you ask.

"Do you know who your neighbor is?" she replies.

"Huh?"

"Your neighbor is a corrections officer at the MCDC."

"The MCDC?"

"The Multnomah County Detention Center," she says. "The prison right here in downtown Portland. It's half a mile from where we're standing right now. It is just one of the many facilities we're targeting for this action."

She continues to explain the plan: coordinated, simultaneous bomb threats to nearly 100 detention centers, jails, prisons, and police stations all across the country. This group is the Portland cell of a larger organization.

"And when they try to determine where these calls came from and who made them," she says. "Each call will have originated from one of their own. For the MCDC, this is your neighbor."

"And how do you expect him to call in a bomb threat?" you ask.

"We don't," she says. "You are."

"No way," you say. "I'm sorry, you have the wrong idea."

"It's easier than you think," she says. "You're friendly with the neighbor. Your family has a spare key. After he leaves for work Monday morning, you'll go into his house and use his landline phone to call the MCDC and say there's a bomb in the building. That's it."

"Oh," you say. "That's all there is to it, huh?"

"You can decide tomorrow," she says. "But tonight you need to think about what you're doing to fight against oppression and this bullshit police state."

"A-C-A-B," shouts one of the others.

"This is crazy," you say. "You're all crazy. I gotta go."

"Crazy is doing nothing!" the leader yells. "Crazy is the

police killing with impunity. Crazy is letting them get away with this! Crazy is business as usual, and ya know what? Business as usual stops now!"

"I'm outta here," you say.

"No one gets hurt," she says. "But they will all suffer."

"Until you get caught," you say.

"We won't get caught," she says. "And if you find yourself unable to sleep tonight thinking of all the atrocities these pigs have committed and you come to realize that you do want to take action, you do want to help, then come back here at this time tomorrow and we'll prepare together."

You look around the group of young people in the cinema. Everyone's looking at you. They look hopeful, but desperate.

"All the best," you say and turn to leave.

"We'll see you tomorrow," someone says.

You pause and smile. Then you leave the room, exit the cinema, mount your bike, and ride home.

That night, Friday, July 12, 2020, you sleep soundly in your childhood bedroom at your parents' home in Portland while 2,600 miles away in Atlanta, Georgia, a 27-year-old man is shot in the back and killed by police officers.

In the morning you see the news: Police were called to a Wendy's fast food restaurant where they found Rayshard Brookes, asleep in his car. After failing a sobriety test, Brookes resisted arrest and attempted to flee on foot when one of the officers shot and killed him.

Why can't the police just not kill people? Why did they shoot this man in the back when he was running away? Why did they even feel the need to arrest him?

Why won't this violence stop? Fuck the police!

You need to do something. Maybe you should join in on the action with those protestors? Then again, you don't want to commit a crime. Maybe there's something else you can do?

You have to do something!

Stay home and donate to the ACLU, turn to page 41.
Return to the cinema and join the action, turn to page 48.

If you ain't going to your friend's BBQ rooftop Memorial Day Party, you sure as hell ain't going to the strange dance party in the street. They probably all have COVID.

You have everything you need right here… Carol Baskin, Joe Exotic, John Finlay, and the rest of the "Tiger King" family.

You binge watch "Tiger King" over and over and over and over and over as your muscles atrophy, and your breath grows short. Days turn to weeks, and then, one evening you close your eyes for sleep and never wake up.

Are you still watching?

You did not survive 2020.

THE END

"We're good," Jimmy says to Quinn. "Ok, thanks, bye!"

Jimmy grabs you by the arm and takes you with him as you walk away. "Screw her," he says. "Whiskey?"

"Sure," you say. Still, you can't help but feel a bit hurt by what Quinn was saying.

You and Jimmy find a friend with a bottle and each take a shot, then another, then another. The wind picks up and it feels great to be drunk, outside, on a rooftop, surrounded by people… the stereo is playing "oh baby" by LCD Soundsystem. You're feeling it, swaying, dancing, everything is great.

For the first time in months you feel happy and free.

Jimmy and another friend are sitting on the parapet of the roof's edge and you join them. Everyone is laughing and telling jokes.

"What did one tampon say to the other tampon?" asks one woman with a big, toothy smile.

"What?" someone else says.

"Nothing!" she says. "They were both stuck up bitches!"

Everyone laughs.

"Rude!" says Jimmy.

"I've got one," you say. "A duck walks into a bar and orders a beer. The bartender serves the duck, who chugs it down, and then asks the bartender, 'got any flies?' The bartender is like, 'What? No, we don't have any flies, what kind of question is that?' The duck shrugs, leaves some money on the bar and walks out. The next day the duck comes back, orders and pays for a beer, chugs it down and asks the bartender again, 'got any flies?' The bartender is annoyed, saying, 'I told you yesterday we ain't got no damn flies. And if you ask me again I'm gonna take a hammer and nail your beak to this here bar, got it?' The duck shrugs and leaves. The next day, the duck comes back, orders a beer, chugs it, and says, 'Hey bartender, got any nails?' The bartender is confused, says, 'No, we don't have any nails, does this look like a hardware store?' 'Well then,' the duck says. 'Got any flies?'"

Some people laugh, painfully.

"That's real bad," Jimmy says.

"This jokester needs another beer!" someone says.

"Catch!" you hear someone say and look up to see a beer can flying through the air towards you. Reaching to catch it, you over extend, sending your weight over the parapet.

Losing your balance, hands out for the beer, you fall off the roof down eight stories hitting the sidewalk with a heavy splat.

You did not survive 2020.

THE END

This is getting weirder and weirder and you want nothing to do with it. It can't be good news, that's for sure. You just want to lay low and get through this pandemic and maybe stay away from the protests for a little while.

You rip up the letter and throw it in the wastebasket.

The shower steam now fills the bathroom and you take your clothes off and get in the shower, letting the hot water wash away all your concerns. Standing there with the water pelting your face, you decide that tomorrow will be different. Tomorrow you'll focus on doing what's best for you.

That night you toss and turn, barely able to sleep, but in the morning you're motivated. You're going to write. You're going to start writing your novel.

It's a beautiful summer day in the Pacific Northwest and you pack laptop and decide to bike to a coffee shop you know with outdoor seating in a big backyard. It'll be perfect.

Biking through the city on such a beautiful day, you can almost forget about the virus, the unrest, and your old life back in New York. This life isn't so bad. In fact, it's pretty good.

Stopped at a street light, you can't help but smile, happy with your new path and the decisions you've made. Best to stay out of it, that's the right thing to do. And it's just an absolutely gorgeous day.

"Hi there," someone says. It's a young, beautiful girl who just pulled up next to you on her bike. She's smiling, which is strange only because she's not wearing a face mask.

"Hello," you reply.

"Such a great day for a bike ride," she says.

You smile, thinking, it really is.

And it's just enough to distract you from the unmarked van pulling up on your other side. Suddenly the van doors open and out jump three large men in ski masks. One grabs you around the chest and clamps his gloved hand across your mouth, pulling you off the bike. Another man grabs your legs and together they pull you into the van.

The last thing you see before they shut the van door is a third man mounting your bike and riding away as the girl on her bike rides away in the opposite direction.

The van lurches forward and one of the men says, “Don’t say a fucking word, got it?”

You nod, scared. The man holding you with his hand across your mouth lets go and zip ties your hands behind your back. The other man covers your head with a black hood.

No one speaks as the van drives through the city. You feel left turns, right turns, breaking at stop lights, but you have no clue where you are or where you’re going or who these men are.

Whether or not you survived 2020 is unknown.

You were never seen again.

THE END

"I should really go," you say. "This has been great, and it was so nice to meet you both."

"You should stay," Jonas says. "Please."

"Thanks," you say. "But I have a FaceTime scheduled for this evening so I should head home."

Quinn skips out with another bottle of champagne and quickly picks up on the situation. "Wait," she says. "You can't leave."

"I wish I could stay, but–" you say.

"But what?" Quinn says.

"But–" you say.

"Just hear us out," Jonas says. "It's important. And you're involved."

"Involved?" you ask. "Involved with what?"

"So now you're curious?" Quinn asks with a smirk.

You can't help but smile. They're weirdos, but they're sweet.

"Please say you'll stay?" Jonas says.

Continue, turn to page 37.

What, you're *not* going to go check out the block party happening outside your apartment? You sure as hell aren't going to sit in your bed listening to it. Even if you just pop down for a minute, you're going.

You throw on some jeans and a t-shirt, adjust your mask, grab your hand sanitizer, and head down to the street. As soon as you exit your building, it hits you like a brick wall: These people are partying!

There's maybe 50 people and a DJ. A couple of people are selling homemade cocktails in plastic bottles from a cooler. The music is great, some kind of samba, super fast and heavy with percussion. It's nearly impossible not to move to it and you find yourself dancing humbly in the perimeter of the dance floor, so to speak.

Soon enough, you're in the mix, letting go, truly enjoying yourself for the first time in months. It's wonderful! And then, out of nowhere, a full-on brass band marches into the party. The DJ takes a break and this band of maybe 10 people playing drums and horns takes the party to the next level. It's incredible.

All of a sudden someone hands you a tambourine and now you're playing along with the band. Everyone is dancing! The band shifts gears into a sort of on and off rhythm, a call and response beat, someone shouts, "Somebody scream!" And the crowd howls!

You've never felt so connected to your neighbors, to all these New Yorkers around you. Even through the masks you can see that everyone is smiling and celebrating this moment.

It's magical.

When the band winds down, the DJ resumes playing, some R&B this time, and the crowd begins to thin.

"Hey," someone says to you. It's a young woman, a trumpet player from the band. "There's another party a few blocks away," she says. "We're heading there if you want to come with!"

"Oh," you say. "That's fun but I should probably turn in. I loved your performance though, thank you!"

"Thanks," she says. "We're heading to DC tomorrow, actually. Raised the money through Venmo doing these kinds of parties, moving around the neighborhood. You were funny with that tambourine. I mean, you were fun, it was good! You should come with us!"

"To DC?" you ask. "Oh no, no, no..."

"Why not?"

"Well..." you say, realizing you don't really have a good reason.

"Come with!" says one of the other brass band members, the tuba player. "That tambourine work was good, we could use that. Get loud!"

You laugh.

"My name is Chloe," the trumpet player says. "This is Beau."

"Nice to meet you," you say, and introduce yourself.

"Listen," Chloe says, pulling out a card from her pocket and writing something on it. "This is my number. We're leaving at noon from Grand Army Plaza. We're just going for a few days, something fun to do. Got an Airbnb. It's safe, we're always safe. And you should join us."

You take the card. It reads BADASS BROOKLYN BRASS BAND. "I'll think about it," you say.

"Yeah, think about it," she says, as Beau calls for her to catch up with the rest of the band who are already on their way. "Hopefully, we'll see you tomorrow."

"We'll see!" you say.

Chloe stands there looking at you. You look at her wondering what to say.

"I'll need that back," she says.

You're still holding the tambourine.

"Oh! Yes, of course," you say, and hand it to her.

"See ya later," Chloe says, trotting off to catch up with the rest of the band.

You hang around for a while as the party dies down and when the DJ starts packing up his gear, you head back into your building.

Entering your apartment, the smell of pot smoke and fajitas still lingers. Your bedroom, what was just earlier a comforting cocoon, now looks like a pigsty.

You collapse onto your bed and realize you haven't had that much fun in a long time, pandemic or otherwise. Dancing, playing the tambourine, being a part of something larger than yourself, was truly transformative.

You go to sleep with a smile on your face.

In the morning you wake up feeling energized and excited. It's a new day! But what to do with it?

You could go to D.C. with that brass band, which would be wild and spontaneous. It's not that crazy though, is it?

Or is it?

Stay in Brooklyn, turn to page 45.
Accept the invite and go to D.C., turn to page 50.

The steam of the bathroom makes it easy to peel open the seal. Inside is a single sheet of folded paper. You unfold it to read:

> *You are in real danger. At risk to my own life, I am reaching out because I can help you. Meet me tonight at midnight at Poets Beach under the Marquam Bridge. Leave your phone at home. Tell no one and destroy this note.*

What the hell is this? Some kind of prank? A weird hazing from those protestors. How do they know where you live? What could you have possibly done to put yourself in "real danger."

In a fit of frustration and confusion, you rip up the letter into tiny pieces and throw it all in the toilet.

After the shower, you head to the kitchen. It's now 10pm and your parents have gone to bed and the house is dark and quiet. You grab some crackers to snack on...

Would those protesters really go so far as to figure out where you live and hand-deliver an ominous note to get you to join their cause? But how could they have even delivered it? The letter was here waiting for you when you got home from their meeting at the cinema. It must be someone else.

But either way, is it legit? Is your life actually in danger? And if it is, why not go and see this person. Then again, it could be a weird trap. Going to the protest meeting without a phone was one thing, but not bringing your phone to a strange meeting under the bridge?

You eat a cracker. And then you eat another one. The sound of your chewing the crispy cracker seems to echo in your brain. The clock reads 10:50pm.

You need to make a decision.

Go to the meeting but bring your phone, turn to page 42.
Go to the meeting without your phone, turn to page 47.
Stay home and ignore the letter, turn to page 58.

"Yeah, sure," you say. "I'll stay, I'm curious."

"Very good," Jonas says. "Quinn, would you mind?"

"Oh," Quinn says. "Yes, of course!" Quinn approaches you. "I'll need to take your phone," she tells you.

"My phone?" you ask.

"Oh, I'll give it back when you leave," Quinn says. "But if we're going to talk any further, I'll need your phone. Don't worry, I just put them in the fridge, it doesn't hurt it."

You hand Quinn your phone.

"Beautiful day," Jonas says, staring off at the splintered sunlight coming through the leaves rustling in the wind.

Quinn returns with a newly opened bottle of champagne and Jonas continues: he explains that the COVID-19 virus was indeed manufactured and while it was not intentionally released – it was an accident – the weapon is built to be exactly as deadly and infectious and asymptomatic as we've seen. Yes, there are many brilliant minds working on a vaccine, but the chances are slim that one will be distributed safely and efficiently before millions more die.

"And you can prove this?" you ask.

"What evidence would convince you?" he asks.

"I don't know," you say. "Maybe some proof that the disease is man made? Who made it?"

"I can access that information," he says. "But I can't do it alone."

Someone else walks out of the house into the garden. Another tall, blonde man with longhair. He looks just like Jonas.

"Hello, brother," Jonas says.

"Amos!" Quinn says, jumping up and giving him a big hug and a very sensual kiss. "Something to drink? This is our new friend."

"Nice to meet you," Amos says. "Will you be joining us?"

"Possibly," says Jonas, answering for you.

"Joining you for what?" you ask.

"I can prove everything that I've told you," Jonas says. "But we need your help."

"My help?"

"The truth of the matter is," Jonas says, with a sigh. "We

will not survive, we are too close, too invested, we know too much. We need someone, we need you, to carry out the last piece of our mission."

"And what would that be exactly?"

"Once we've obtained the evidence," Jonas says. "You deliver it to the press, a reporter who will be waiting for you."

"Whoa, whoa, whoa..." you say, laughing. "This is a bit much."

Amos pulls up a chair and sits next to Jonas. They're clearly identical twins. "What is your goal in life?" Amos asks.

"What?"

"What do you want to do with your life?" Amos says. "Do you want to make money and have a family? Do you want to create a legacy of work that lives on when you're gone? Do you want to live free and easy, enjoying life's pleasures?"

"All of these paths are completely acceptable," Jonas says.

"Or do you want to take an opportunity to do something truly incredible?" Amos asks. "Something that actually matters? Something that is righteous and good?"

"Look," you say. "I'm interested in what you're saying, I do think it's interesting, but honestly I don't think I can help you."

"You don't want to help," Jonas says.

"You choose not to believe because the truth is too painful," Amos says.

"Ok, look," you say. "I'm happy to help you but I don't even know what you want me to do? Deliver some kind of evidence to some journalist somewhere? Why me?"

"Because he'll trust you," Jonas says.

"Trust me?"

"It's Elliott," says Quinn.

"What?"

"Elliott Sutherland," Jonas says. "We want you to deliver the evidence to–"

"Who the hell are you guys?" you ask. "What the hell is going on here?"

"We need your help," says Quinn.

"No," you say. "This is just too much. I don't know you. I don't know what I'm doing here. I'm leaving, I need to leave."

You stand. "I would like my phone back please."

"Of course," Jonas says.

"Just so you know," Amos says. "Elliott is not involved. But I think you'll agree that he's the best person to deliver this information to the public."

"You guys are crazy," you say. "This is crazy."

"We can make sure that no one ever knows about what you and Elliott–"

"Shut up," you say. "You Children-of-the-Corn-looking, giant viking motherfuckers. Where's my phone, I'm leaving."

"Ok," Quinn says, and follows you into the kitchen. She leads you to the large stainless steel refrigerator. "It's likely no one will ever know about what you did. But wouldn't it be best if you knew for sure, if you could rest easy knowing you're safe. And do some good at the same time?"

Quinn opens the refrigerator and the sunlight reflecting off the steel door blinds you and triggers a flashback: you and Elliott and two others dressed all in black placing explosive devices in a darkened office building. You had planned the action as part of the Animal Liberation Front and burned down the Reno, Nevada office building of Scientific Resources International, a company that imports primates from China for scientific research. While no one was injured, those actions caused over $300,000 in damages. This was a couple of years ago but if you're caught the four of you could face charges of arson, maybe worse.

You snap back to the present moment with Quinn holding out your phone. You grab it.

"That was a long time ago," you say.

"If not for yourself," Quinn says. "Do it for Elliott. He could lose his career, everything he's worked so hard for."

"Screw you."

"It's just an incentive," Quinn says. "You help us, we can help you."

You look at your phone: three missed calls from your father and three other calls from another Portland, Oregon number, but no voicemails.

"I got to go," you say, and leave without looking back.

Outside, in front of the building, it's now twilight. You call your father and he answers right away. You can tell something is wrong before he even speaks. "Your mother is sick," he says and you crumble to sit on the stoop. He says she's tested positive for COVID-19 and is currently hospitalized on oxygen. It's all going to be ok, he tells you as he coughs. He should have his test results in a couple of days, but he feels fine. Mom is doing ok. And he says he'll keep you posted.

"Should I fly home?" you ask.

"No," he says. "They won't let you in the hospital. Anyway, I'll call again later."

A cold breeze blows and you burst into tears. You weep on the cold stoop steps of that house for who knows how long. At some point Quinn comes out and sits beside you. It's comforting. The last thing you want to do is go home and be alone. She invites you inside, sets you up with a blanket and a pillow on the couch. Makes you some tea. Jonas and Amos are nowhere to be seen. You finally fall asleep with Quinn sitting, reading on the opposite couch.

In the morning you awake to the smell of coffee and the sounds of cooking from the kitchen. Your phone is on the table next to you: no missed calls. It's still early in Portland, you think. You sit up and rub your face.

If this disease, this virus, takes your mother, someone is going to pay. Hell, it's already taken so many mothers, and fathers, and brothers, and sisters, daughters and sons... if this is actually government-made, the world deserves to know. Why would these people lie about any of this?

And how do they know about Reno and Elliott? Then again, you don't have to get involved. You have no reason to trust them. The coffee smells good but you could just slip out the front door unnoticed.

Sneak out, turn to page 46.
Help them, turn to page 55.

You know what? It's a crazy plan and it's a felony. You can't get mixed up with these radicals, no way.

You pull out your phone and make a donation to the ACLU. Then you make a donation to the Atlanta Solidarity Fund. Feels good, man.

After making yourself some eggs and toast for breakfast, you scroll Instagram for an hour, then check out Twitter for about an hour. Then you go to the New York Times and read a couple of articles before you move back to your bed with your laptop and spend the rest of the day binge watching "The Last Dance."

You've survived 2020. So what?

THE END

After finishing the whole box of crackers, you decide to go. It's after 11pm but that's plenty of time to bike down to Poets Beach. Maybe there's some merit to the letter. And if not, and it's just a prank, well, worst case, you'll be embarrassed.

But there's no way you're not bringing your phone.

You're still thinking it over, maybe just keep it in Airplane Mode, or maybe you'll try to use it to record the audio of your meeting, or maybe not, but you're bringing it, that's for sure.

What else should you bring?

You grab a flashlight, the big one from the garage, it's heavy and would certainly hurt if you hit someone with it.

You write a note to your parents that reads, "Be back in the morning." But you rethink that. Either you'll be back before they see the note or... something's gone wrong. You crumple up the note and throw it in the trash.

It's time to go. You sneak out and bike downtown.

When you roll up on Poets Beach, the place looks empty. You take your time, scouting out the area a bit, but it's dark and the only sound you can hear is the gentle lapping of the river against the shore.

You dismount your bike and walk it down the concrete pathway along the shore towards the bridge. You have the big flashlight in the pouch of your hoodie and – oh, right, the phone! You quickly turn on Airplane Mode and continue cautiously down the path.

Then you see someone. He's facing the river with his back turned to you but it looks like a man, skinny, wearing a trench coat and a fedora. You look up and down the river and see no one else. Slowly, you approach him walking your bike making sure he can hear you. But he doesn't turn. And you stop short keeping a good distance from him.

"It's good that you came," the man says, slowly turning to face you. He's well dressed and the fedora casts a shadow on his face. "We don't have much time now so I need you to listen very carefully to what I'm about to tell you," he says. "The people I work for are very powerful, and very smart, and we've been watching COVID very closely. Despite what the media says, it will be extremely difficult to make a vaccine for this virus. And millions more will die. But there are some people, not many, but some people who have an unexplained immunity to the virus. And we believe those people are our best chance at beating this. But there are others... dangerous parties, who are also pursuing this path..." his voice trails off as if he's distracted by something.

Now you're feeling a bit spooked. "What's all this got to do with me," you ask.

"You have the immunity," he says flatly. "Our AI has combed through millions of blood samples and you are one of the lucky ones."

Suddenly, you hear a car engine from downriver. In the distance you can see a black van barreling down the riverside pathway towards you.

"They found us," the man says.

The van speeds up, heading straight for you.

"Run!" the man says, as he takes off along the pathway up river.

You mount your bicycle and peddle after him and quickly ride past him.

"Run!" he screams.

You peddle as hard as you can and the flashlight falls out of your hoodie pouch and hits the ground with a crack.

You look back at the precise moment that the speeding van plows over the running man. "No!" you scream, and looking forward again you're blinded by the headlines of another van heading towards you. You swerve and dump the bike, sliding along the concrete pathway and off into the sand and gravel of the beach.

You're dazed, with blurred vision, but you hear the van doors open and close then the footsteps of a few people walking towards you. As you roll over and make it to all fours, you can see two pairs of black boots stepping close to you and stopping. You look up at the men but they're backlit by the headlights of their van.

They're speaking to each other but you don't understand the language. Russian maybe?

"Hey dummy," one of the men says to you in English. "Shoulda left your phone at home."

He then pulls out a pistol and shoots you twice in the head.

You did not survive 2020.

THE END

Sure, you'll go to D.C. with a brass band you met on the street. Yeah right! That's just not going to happen, not with the pandemic. You'll stay in your apartment where it's safe.

You have some coffee, maybe too much coffee, and suddenly feel like your apartment is a disgusting mess. And maybe it is. Furiously, you start cleaning. You scrub the kitchen counters, the oven surface, the kitchen table, the sink, inside the microwave. You sweep. You mop. You move on to the bathroom.

You're inside the bathtub scrubbing the brown stains around the drain but it's not cleaning it enough so you get some bleach and go back at it. You turn on the faucet and rinse, then more bleach, more scrubbing. Suddenly you feel a bit lightheaded and stand to take a break but you slip and fall backwards hitting your head on the sink on your way down.

Unconscious, with a fractured skull, you bleed out right there on your bathroom floor.

You did not survive 2020.

THE END

This is too much, you've got to go. With your shoes in your hand you quietly tiptoe to the front door. Carefully, you turn the door knob, and slowly open the door. You step out and as you close the door behind you, you see Quinn standing in the living room watching you leave. You freeze for a moment as your eyes connect: her's say don't go and your's say I'm sorry. You close the door.

Quickly you put on your shoes and walk away, down the sidewalk, back towards your apartment.

Over the next three days you barely leave your bed. You clutch your phone waiting for updates from your father between bouts of nightmare-filled sleep and uncontrollable crying. Your mother's condition remains the same, but somehow you feel worse each day.

In the middle of the night you wake up in a cold sweat. Your bed sheets are soaked. You feel simultaneously very hot and very cold. You cough just a bit but then it seems like you can't stop coughing. Looking at yourself in the bathroom mirror, your skin is pale and your eyes look worse than sad. They look sick.

You drink some water and get back into bed. Eventually you fall asleep and dream that you're drowning. When you wake up, you can barely breathe. This is bad, really bad. It's as if there's a vice clamp around your chest and every movement is difficult. You feel delirious.

Everything that happens next is a blur, events seen through a dark fog: you call 911, you're on a gurney getting carried down the stairs of your apartment building, you arrive at the hospital, bright white lights. The doctors are attacking you! You try to fight them off but cannot.

You're intubated in the intensive care unit of the hospital. Sleeping and waking moments blur. Time moves like slime.

In just a few days, you succumb to the disease, dying alone, helpless and scared.

You did not survive 2020.

THE END

Let's do this, you decide. You'll play along. The letter already says your life is in danger so what do you have to lose?

You dress all in black, and ride your bike to the park, Poets Beach. You stash your bike in bushes near the concrete pathway along the shore just in case you need to make a quick getaway. And then you find a nice spot to stakeout the area under the bridge. It can't be much later than 11:30pm but that's just a guess, really. It feels weird not having a phone.

Tme passes slowly when you have no idea what time it is while hiding in the bushes near a secret meetup location waiting to see if the person who wrote you an anonymous letter shows up. You really should get a watch.

Then, just when you're about to give up, you hear something, like a car engine. But it sounds like it's coming from the river? You stay hidden, waiting. And sure enough, a small outboard motor boat floats toward the shore right under the bridge.

As the boat gets closer you can see two men on board. One is wearing a baseball cap. They cut the engine to glide into the water just between the two bridge pylons where they can hide in the bridge's shadow.

But then nothing. They're just sitting there. Now what?

Do you wait for them to come ashore? Just stay hidden until they call out to you? Or do you make your presence known? Slowly crawl out from the bushes and approach them? You don't want them to think you didn't show up, do you?

Reveal yourself and approach them, turn to page 62.
Wait for their signal, turn to page 70.

Something has to be done. You can't just sit back and watch.

You decide to do a quick bit of reconnaissance that afternoon and ask your mother if the neighbors have keys to the house, "Ya know," you say. "In case we get locked out."

"Yes, of course," your mother says. "They have a set of our keys and we have a set of their's. We keep them in that tin can in the pantry."

That night you return to the cinema and meet with your new compatriots. No phones, no names, no new friends.

Everyone knows what their role is and everything seems to be in order and timed out perfectly: your neighbor will leave for work at 8:15am as always, you'll then enter his house with the spare key, and use his land line in the kitchen to call the MCDC and issue the threat.

"We're counting on you," the leader says.

You nod, saying, "I won't let you down."

The next morning, you're up early and waiting quietly when you hear your neighbor's car door shut. Then you hear the car engine start, and, looking out your window, you watch your neighbor drive away. It's 8:20am. And you take the spare key from the tin can in the pantry.

The target time for the call is 9:45am, to sync with all the other calls. For now, you wait. Time passes slowly. Your parents both wake up and your dad sits to read and drink his coffee while your mother does her morning exercises, beginning with an hour walk on the treadmill.

Ok, 9:40am, time to make this happen. You wear all black, with a black health mask, a black ball cap low on your head, and a pair of black gloves. You look suspicious perhaps but not alarming? Or so you hope.

You go out the back door of your parents' house, across the small yard, over the low rockwall terrace, and into the backyard of your neighbor's house from where you move quickly along the side of the house to the front door.

You enter the key into the lock, turn, and open the door.

But before you step in, you hesitate. You pause for just a moment, at the threshold, before illegally entering someone's house and using their phone to call in a fake bomb threat at a county facility that houses hundreds of detainees and prisoners with hundreds of guards and employees.

Are you sure you want to go through with this?

Are you ready for what consequences may come?

Yes, enter the house and make the call, turn to page 59.
No, call it off and go back home, turn to page 72.

A trip to D.C. with a strange group of street musicians? Yeah, right!

You go about your morning, have some coffee, make some breakfast, you scroll your newsfeeds and read about the police killing a man in Minneapolis. A grocery store clerk called the police after a man allegedly bought a pack of cigarettes with a counterfeit bill. The cops arrived and moved quickly to violently arrest him. As the police held him down on the asphalt, he called for help, begged for help, cried out for his mother, and said the words "I can't breathe" more than 20 times. He was unarmed, in handcuffs, and the police suffocated him with a chokehold, killing him in the street. His name was George Floyd.

You put your phone down and cry quietly in the stillness of the early morning. You feel small. You don't want to be alone. You decide you're going to D.C.

You pack a small bag with some clothes, your phone charger, all the masks you have, a can of Lysol, and some hand sanitiser. You water the one half-dead plant you have and head out, locking the door behind you.

From your apartment to Grand Army Plaza is maybe an hour walk and you debate taking the train but it's only 10AM.

You have time. And you set off walking.

Along the way, you really take in the city, all the empty storefronts, the restaurant seating in the streets, the panhandlers, the roaming packs of teenagers… everything is still here, all the things that were here before the pandemic, but at the same time it's completely different. It's like a nightclub with the house lights turned on showing all the trash left behind after the party. It's like an empty goldfish bowl. It's like a classic, antique car up on cinder blocks. You can't help but feel like you're walking through the aftermath of a great flood with people gathering found materials building what they can, scavenging what remains, and trying to live a life that feels normal, a life "before all this."

Coming up on Grand Army Plaza at the entrance to Prospect Park, you make a conscious decision not to dwell on the negative side of things and focus on what's next, stay positive: you're going to have fun on this trip! If only unofficially, temporarily, you're part of the BADASS BROOKLYN BRASS BAND.

You see a minibus parked at the park entrance so you make your way there and find Chloe and Beau and the rest of the band hanging out, packing their things into the back of the bus.

"Well, shit," Chloe says when she sees you. "Look who showed up."

"I figured why not?" you say.

"You figured right, I'll say that!" says Beau.

"Ok, y'all," announces an older man holding a clipboard. "All aboard who's going aboard."

And one by one all of you step onto the bus and find a seat. There's at least 15 of you and at first you think there may not be enough room for everyone but then find yourself sitting on your own.

The bus right is somber, just quiet talk about the murder of George Floyd. But when Beau assigns himself DJ duties, the last half of the ride is a good time.

You arrive at the Airbnb and the house is huge, plenty of room. Social distancing is pretty much out the window, taking the bus, sharing a house, but you move on quickly. That evening the band hangs out together, cooking dinner, and you meet the rest of the group. Everyone is so pleasant and happy and you even forget about the pandemic for a while.

But now more news of George Floyd's murder has come out and whispered discussions turn to angry conversations. Everyone in the house is upset.

That night it's agreed to stay in and rest, but there's big plans for the rest of the week, and while the plan is for the bus to drive everyone back to Brooklyn on Saturday, it seems that some of the band members are planning to stay longer.

The next day everyone pairs off to explore the city. You go solo and just walk and walk and walk, visiting the major landmarks, getting a sandwich to go and eating it on the steps of the Lincoln Memorial. That evening you head back to the house where there's another group dinner before you all set out to march and perform in the streets.

"Here we go, y'all!" Beau announces, leading the band

out of the house and down the street.

Immediately, you're impressed by the amount of people in the streets. This isn't the playful springtime dance parties you've seen in Brooklyn. This is protest. This is purpose.

"Whose streets?"

"OUR STREETS!"

People are chanting and singing songs while marching. Everyone's wearing masks and carrying signs. It feels like the entire city is in the streets. You're excited to be part of it. And then the band begins and you chime in with your tambourine and nothing could be better. Getting loud, making music, protesting police brutality and the toxic administration, you've never been this vocal or political but it feels fantastic.

"This is great," you say to Chloe.

She nods, wide-eyed, playing her trumpet.

You make your way, block by block, gathering more and more people, protestors, dancers... The crowd starts to swell and grow thick. You're now packed shoulder to shoulder. The chants and singing give way to shouts and screams. Ahead of you there's a commotion, maybe a fight? You can't quite tell. The band stops playing, one instrument at a time. And for a moment, there's a quiet stillness. The crowd is stagnant.

Suddenly people are pushing, running, falling down, it's chaos. You can smell a strong chemical in the air. Your fight or flight instincts kick in, but you're stuck in the middle of it all.

The crowd groans and undulates. People are screaming. You're pushed one way then another, and now you're completely cut off from the rest of the band. A young man pushes past you screaming, "Medic!"

Others are following behind him, some screaming in pain with eyes closed and others helping those along. You jump in behind them and follow through the crowd and out into an open space on a street corner.

A dozen men and women sit or kneel on the sidewalk some screaming in pain, all of them suffering from mace and teargas from police at the front line of the crowd. Medics and others work to aid them with plastic bottles of milky liquid they pour on their faces and into their eyes.

You survey the scene: the crowd swells behind you as some run out and others run in. A white cloud of gas hovers and dissipates at the front. You scan the crowd for your band-mates but see no one.

"Water!" someone screams. "We need water!"

You jolt and flinch as fireworks explode in the crowd. Police sirens sound in the distance. You stand there, still holding your tambourine, confused, angry, and scared.

"Hey!" you hear a woman say and she grabs your arm. It's Chloe. "We gotta get out of here."

Together you make your way out of the area, walking through an otherwise calm and untouched Washington D.C., so clean and proper, a dark contrast to the chaotic protest and clashes you're escaping.

You walk back to the Airbnb house without speaking much, and find that you're the first ones home.

"No one else is back yet?" Chloe says, standing in the kitchen. You shrug, not sure what to say.

Suddenly Chloe starts to cry and you embrace each other.

You hear the door open. "Hello?" Beau calls.

"In here," Chloe replies.

Beau and Chloe embrace. "Glad you're ok," Beau says.

The rest of the band returns to the house in pairs or one at a time and soon enough everyone is home and accounted for and dinner is prepared. The conversations on the protests are strange, somehow both pointed and hollow.

Some are worried things will escalate and some are ready to instigate escalation. All are sad and angry, and some are determined to do something about it, take to the streets, make their voices heard.

By the end of the evening, the band has decisively divided itself into two groups: those who are returning early to Brooklyn in the van, and those who are pooling their money to extend the Airbnb reservation through Monday and then taking the train back to New York.

You support the Black Lives Matter movement and believe in public protest and civil disobedience, but you're out of your comfort zone here in D.C.. And you can't help but feel like things may get violent. Or worse, what if you contract COVID while in the crowds of protestors?

This is a different trip now than the one you initially embarked on. You want justice for George Floyd and you're willing to fight, but maybe it's best to head back home to Brooklyn as planned.

Then again, what if you stayed?

Take the bus back home to Brooklyn, turn to page 63.
Stay in D.C. through the weekend, turn to page 83.

You're not sure how, or how much they know about Reno, but it's enough to make you want to believe the other stuff they've said.

You enter the kitchen and find Jonas and Amos and Quinn all together cooking breakfast: vegetable skillet, waffles, sliced fruit. The sun is shining in from the garden.

"Coffee?" Quinn asks, handing you a mug of black coffee.

The four of you sit to eat and surprisingly the small talk isn't uncomfortable. When it seems like everyone is finished eating, Jonas says, "I'm glad you decided to stay with us. And I'm sorry to hear about your mother. I believe she will recover, I really do. And for her, and for all the others who will not recover from COVID, that is why we need to do what we've set out to do."

He holds out his hand for your phone and you give it to him. He then takes Quinn's phone and Amos's phone and with his own puts them all inside the refrigerator.

Together, Amos and Jonas explain the plan: there's a lab, a secret laboratory, disguised as a film stage on the Brooklyn waterfront. The weeknight security guard is a friend and ready to help, but he doesn't know what to look for. Once inside, Amos will hack into the computer system and Jonas will gather the materials and information, which will then be handed off to you to take directly to Elliott Sutherland at his apartment in Clinton Hill, conveniently just a mile away. We'll leave by car, the same way we arrive, but we won't leave together. You'll travel to Elliott's by bicycle.

"More coffee?" asks Quinn.

"What if you can't find what you're looking for?" you ask.

"We will," Jonas says.

"What if you can't hack into the system?" you ask.

"I can," Amos says.

"As soon as we come out, you take the harddrive, hop on the bike, and we go our separate ways."

"When are you planning for this?"

The three each take turns looking at each other.

"Tonight?" Quinn says with a smile.

The day passes in a daze. You speak with your father

twice, but he has no new information: your mother is hospitalized but not intubated. And he's still waiting for his results.

Jonas and Amos show you schematics for the laboratory. You run through the operation, the entrance, the theft, the exit, biking the straight shot path to Sutherland's house.

You haven't seen Elliott Sutherland in over 10 years. But you're excited most about that. He's become quite a renowned journalist, certainly the most successful of your old ALF crew.

The night goes on, passing midnight, and then, as if all of a sudden, "It's time," Jonas says.

You dress as technicians with white jumpsuits, reflective vests, gloves, and of course medical masks and safety goggles. The van is white and clean, looks brand new.

The four of you climb into the van, which is empty save for the black mountain bike. Jonas drives you south and takes the Manhattan Bridge over the East River. From the bridge, you turn right onto Navy Street, then left onto Park Avenue, driving along the underbelly of the Brooklyn Queens Expressway. You're the only car on the road. Then left onto Cumberland Street.

Amos says, "One minute."

Everyone takes a deep breath, and exchanges looks to say, yes, we're ready.

The van rolls to a stop at the streetlight at Flushing and Cumberland with the Navy Yard entrance straight ahead. As soon as the van stops, you jump out. Quinn hands you the bicycle, and you quickly lock it to a street sign pole, and then you're back in the van. The light changes Jonas drives across Flushing Avenue into the gated Navy Yard towards the guard booth.

Jonas stops the van a bit before the booth and we wait for the guard to appear. He ambles up to the van with a flashlight and a walkie talkie and asks, "Can I help you?"

Jonas rolls down his window and says something in Swedish.

"What's that?" the guard asks, approaching.

Jonas has something in his hand.

At the van window, the guard asks, ""Can I help you?"

In one fluid movement Jonas is halfway out the window and stabs the man in the neck. Amos hops out the passenger side and trots around in front of the van to catch the guard as he stumbles backwards. You can see the syringe sticking out of the guard's neck as he tries to speak and loses consciousness while Amos drags him back into the guard booth.

"What the hell?" you say.

"It's too late to go back now," Quinn says.

You stay quiet, shocked, not sure what your options are.

Amos zip ties the guard in the booth, takes the guard's keycard, and pushes the button to open the gate.

Now he's back in the van and Jonas drives through the gate, then a left around one building, then a right around another building, and finally parking at the back of a small, discreet building with a loading dock.

Jonas and Amos jump out of the van.

"Are you coming?" Quinn says. "We're safer together."

This wasn't part of the plan. They lied about having someone on the inside of the facility. But now maybe it's too late? If you run, then what? There's Reno. And who knows what may happen if you go out on your own right now. But maybe it's best to bail.

Go inside with them, turn to page 66.
Bail and run for it, turn to page 74.

It's not worth the weirdness. Or the risk. Whatever joker planted that letter in your mailbox surely doesn't have your best interests in mind. After all… the virus, the protests, stranger danger, yeah, it's best to just stay home, stay safe.

You finish your crackers and get ready for bed. Cuddling up with your laptop, you stream a movie, a classic from your childhood. You feel safe and comfortable. At some point you notice the time: 12:22am.

Well, the opportunity is over now. You rest assured.

Eventually, in the glow of your laptop screen, you drift off to sleep.

Continue, turn to page 77.

Let's do this. You quickly enter the house and closethe door behind you.

You move silently through the house to the kitchen where you find the phone. You dial the number you memorized last night and reach the automated phone menu greeting. You press the number 0 and listen as the phone rings connecting you.

"MCDC," a man says. "How may I direct your call."

"Listen carefully," you say, just as instructed. "There is a bomb in the building that will explode in fifteen minutes. You need to evacuate immediately."

"What?" the man says.

"You have fifteen minutes before the bomb explodes," you say and hang up.

You move quickly through the house, out the door, lock it behind you, jog across the backyards and into your parents' house. You return the key to the tin in the pantry. And you figure why not just disrobe everything, pack it in a bag to dispose of later, and take a shower.

You did it, man. Screw the cops. Let them panic and freak out for a day, ain't hurting nobody really. Oh man, the looks on their faces when they have to bring in some sort of search team and find nothing.

Now dressed after your shower you pass through the living room on your way to the kitchen to make some breakfast and find your parents both transfixed on the television.

Breaking news: "Dozens are confirmed dead in an apparent terrorist bombing in downtown Portland, Oregon this morning," a newscaster announuces over video of the bombed out MCDC facade.

"Oh no," you say.

"They're saying there's been about a dozen of these bombings along the west coast," your dad says.

"It wasn't supposed to be real," you mutter.

"That's where George next door works," your mom says.

"I'm going for a ride," you say.

"Oh, ok," your mom says. "See you for dinner?"

"Yeah," you say and head out.

It's probably not the smartest idea to head to the cinema but you don't know what else to do. They must have planned real bombs this whole time. They lied to you. They used you.

You ride into downtown Portland faster than you ever have. You stop at a street light and realize your hands are white and cramped from holding the handlebars so tightly. You're enraged.

A flurry of cop cars, sirens blaring, speed past the intersection. Maybe you'll just turn them in. Better them than you, right? You had no idea what they were really planning. But you're not a snitch. Or maybe this is the exception?

You ride along 5th Avenue and slowly pass the cinema. From what you can tell, it's quiet, empty. You stop at the next intersection. Should you lock up your bike and check inside the cinema? What if it's being watched? What if the police are waiting?

Then, you see her down the alley behind the cinema: the leader of the group closing the back doors of a large, purple van. You see another one of the group members walking from the backdoor of the cinema towards the van carrying a duffle bag. Wait, is that them?

Yeah, it's them. You bike over as the man with the duffle bag gets in the van and shuts the side door. The leader is opening the door to the driver's seat. "All set?" she says to the people inside the van.

"Hey," you say, startling her.

"Jesus," she says. "What're you doing here? Are you ok?"

"No," you say. "I'm not ok! That was a real bomb! You really bombed them."

"Don't," she says. "Don't use that kind of language."

"Screw you!"

"I can understand how you would be upset right now," she says. "But you need to listen to me, ok? We're leaving. We're leaving right now and we're never coming back. And you should come with us."

"What!" someone exclaims from inside the van.

"Leaving for where?" you ask.

"Someplace safe," she says. "We're in danger if we stay."

"No shit," you say.

"This isn't a joke!" she says. "You can leave right now, with us, and we can protect you. Or you can stay here. And you're on your own."

"I can't trust you!" you say.

She just looks at you.

"You killed innocent people!" you say.

She just looks at you.

You hear police sirens in the distance.

"Come with us," she says.

You're an accomplice, undoubtedly. But do you run away with these terrorists in their getaway van? What then? What about your parents? Or do you let them leave and bike home like nothing happened? Either way, will you be safe?

Get in the van and leave with them, turn to page 88.
Take your chances on your own, turn to page 96.

The ball has been in your court since you got the letter. It's up to you to make the next move.

You stand up out of the bushes and slowly make your way toward the shore. The two men see you almost instantly, and the one in the baseball cap excitedly jumps out of the boat into the knee-deep water. Wading in the water, he pulls the boat towards the shore waving at you. You wave back.

"We have to hurry," he says as you get closer to the waterline. "Get in the boat."

"Where are we going?" you ask.

"I'll explain everything on the way, but we need to go," he says. "We need to go now."

"I'm not going anywhere until you tell me where we're going."

"Seattle," he says, curtly. "Let's go, let's go!"

"In that?" you ask. "You're not going to get to Sea–"

"We will both die here if you don't get in this boat right now," he says.

Get in the boat, turn to page 93.

Insist on more information, turn to page 100.

In many ways, it's just better to go home. No good would come of staying in D.C., protesting, spending money you don't have on the house. The plan was to come down for a few days to play music but things are different now. It's time to go home.

Everyone on the bus is silent for the entire ride back to Brooklyn. You read the news on your phone about increasing protests, property damage, "riots", and now the weekend is scary with everyone bracing for what's next.

From Grand Army Plaza you once again make the long walk back to your apartment. The city now seems worse for wear with retail and restaurants now fully boarded up, graffiti-riddled plywood covering all the windows. You wonder if there are actually windows underneath the plywood, or if the windows have already been broken. Does it matter?

Back home you sit at your kitchen table with nothing to do, nowhere to go, no idea what will come next.

The protests and riots escalate. Looters ransack stores in Times Square and Union Square. Mayor Bill DeBlasio institutes a city-wide 8pm curfew, the first of its kind since 1943, when Mayor Fiorello LaGuardia issued an emergency curfew in response to an uprising in Harlem sparked by a white police officer shooting a black soldier.

Protests roil through the city during the day and clash with police in the evenings. Hundreds are arrested. The police continue to assault and attack citizens protesting police brutality.

You can't sleep. If it's not the incessant fireworks, it's the hovering police helicopters that keep you up all night, every night.

In Seattle, a man drives his car into a crowd of protesters while shooting at people, prompting protestors to create a perimeter of their occupied area calling it the Capitol Hill Autonomous Zone then renamed the Capitol Hill Organized Protest. Additional shootings and violence occur over the next weeks until organizers agree to leave and the area is cleared.

The coronavirus continues to plague the US. Despite all lockdown efforts on the east coast and western US, over a dozen states are seeing increases in COVID cases and deaths.

Each morning you wake up and read what feels like doomsday worldnews. China's national security law passes now with jurisdiction over Hong Kong to enforce vague, totalitarian laws. Locusts, literally swarms of locusts, plague parts of Delhi, India. In Russia, 20,000 gallons of fuel spills into a river in Norilsk with catastrophic environmental damage. Militant terrorists in Nigeria attack a village killing over 80 people and kidnapping others. The Lebanese currency tanks as citizens take to the streets of Beirut for anti-government protests.

This is June, 2020.

You can't read the news without crying.

The impending Fourth of July holiday feels ominous and downright evil. How could we celebrate ourselves at this moment?

Most nights, lying awake in your bed, you imagine aliens from another planet arriving to Earth to fix all this madness.

Then, one night, as if you need more distractions from sleep, you hear footsteps on the roof of your building. Your top floor apartment does not have much between your ceiling and the rooftop so any footsteps sound like thunder, like, a parade on the roof. But this? This sounds almost like a party. Who the hell is having a party on the roof!

Frustrated, you clamour out of bed, throw on some pants and shoes and take the hallway ladder up and out through the roof hatch. And it is a damn party! There's probably a dozen of your neighbors up there just hanging out. As you walk to approach them and reprimand them for being on the roof you realize that they're not really hanging out or talking with each other at all. They're all just standing there staring off into the distance. And then you see what everyone is looking at: hovering low over Manhattan are four massive objects, dark and silver with some dim flashing lights. There's no denying it. They're UFOs.

"Wild, huh?" one of your neighbors says.

"What is happening?" you ask.

"No one knows," he says. "They just showed up. Here, DC, LA, London, Paris, Moscow, all over the world." He shows you his phone and on the screen there's a New York Times "breaking news" article that reads "Unidentified Flying Objects Appear Over World's Cities."

You stand there stupefied. Did you somehow predict this? Or manifest this? Who are they? What are they?

"The Russians said they've made contact," your neighbor says. "Unreal..."

You head back down to your room, pull out your laptop, and ravenously read anything and everything you can, all the breaking news, watch all the videos, all the pundits rousted from their beds to report on "the next chapter of humanity, first contact with extraterrestrial life."

You feel bad for those folks who are sleeping through this moment, but wow – what a thing to wake up to!

The news from Russia is that there will be a press briefing at 10am Moscow time, which is 3am New York time. Fantastic, there's no way you're going to miss this.

There's not much more news otherwise, it seems that the crafts are stationary and while the government and local police have attempted to keep a perimeter underneath the crafts that's been nearly impossible. Reports indicate the estimated size of these things and the one over Manhattan, directly above Central Park, is almost a mile wide.

Some are looting again like earlier in the month, while others are heading towards the crafts, like pilgrims, ready to welcome the extraterrestrials. You imagine others descending to their bunkers. Governments worldwide report their world leaders are in safe, secured locations, whatever than means.

Should you go over there? Head to Central Park and see the craft up close? Or better to stay put and see what the press briefings have to say? If what Russia says is true, and they've made contact, that 3am briefing could be major. But, why would you sit at home when you could go to the UFOs?

Then again, do you really want to get closer?

Stay home and wait for the press briefings, turn to page 90.
Head to Central Park to see the UFOs, turn to page 98.

There's just no way you're going to stay in the van. You follow Quinn behind Jonas and Amos and watch Amos use the keycard to open the external door. You enter the building and follow them behind a long, dimly lit corridor, passing a number of doors with small viewing windows along one side.

At the end of the corridor is another door. Amos uses the keycard and then types in a code on a keypad. The door opens. You follow and enter a larger, square room, also dimly lit, lined with desks and tables holding computers and laboratory equipment. You can't tell why, but something is strange about the walls of the room.

Amos kneels on the floor in front of one of the computers, connects a piece of hardware he brought with him, and powers on the computer.

"Seventy-five seconds," Jonas says. He's watching the door through which you came.

Amos has the computer online and is typing away in the terminal.

You step backwards pressing against one of the tables.

"Stay in the center of the room," Quinn tells you. She looks nervous.

You move back towards the center of the room. Looking at the walls again – are they windows? Black glass?

"Forty-five seconds," Jonas says.

"Almost there," Amos answers.

Jonas looks at Quinn.

"He'll get it," Quinn says. "Be ready." She takes out a GoPro camera from the pocket of her jumpsuit. Jonas also pulls out a GoPro camera.

You realize you haven't been breathing and take a deep breath.

"Thirty-five seconds!" Jonas says.

Suddenly, the room lights up with bright fluorescent lights in the ceiling

"Got it!" Amos says, unplugging his hardware and stepping away from the computer. Among the computers and equipment is some kind of control station with a microphone on a bendable stand and three sets of switches and buttons.

"Rolling," Quinn says, aiming her camera at one of the walls.

"Rolling," Jonas says, aiming his camera at the opposite wall.

Amos mans the control station and flips a switch. It triggers one of the strange glass walls to suddenly go clear. He pushes another button that lights the room behind the glass. Inside the room is a seemingly normal studio apartment with two beds, one with a sleeping man and one with a sleeping woman. They awake and shield their eyes from the bright light, straining to see through the glass.

Amos flips the switch and pushes the button of the other set that changes the massive glass wall from opaque to clear but inside is not another studio prison holding a couple. The room is white and barren save for a large green man, a muscly lizard of sorts, a reptilian humanoid, naked and without genitalia, standing very close to the glass looking out at you.

Quinn gasps.

"Keep rolling," Amos says.

"Hey," the man in the studio says, his voice heard not through the glass but through speakers in the control room. "Hey, who are you?"

The woman, wearing a nightgown, climbs from her bed and approaches the window. "Hello? Hello! Oh my god, they're here to help us!"

Amos, using the microphone, speaks to the man and woman in the studio: "Tell us your names, and how long you've been here."

"My name is Chelsea Muir," says the woman.

"I'm Eric Ronan," says the man. But then they look at each other, unsure. "We think we've been here for maybe two months. Since February?"

"Please," says the woman. "Can you help us! Before they come back."

"You're very brave," you hear a voice say. "But you can't save them."

"Are you getting this?" Amos asks Jonas and Quinn.

"It's telepathic," says Jonas, aiming his camera at the

reptilian humanoid now standing right against the glass. Its eyes are yellow and its mouth is wide.

"They're coming," the voice says.

"We have to help them!" says Quinn.

"What have you experienced here?" asks Amos through the microphone. "Who is keeping you here?"

"They say they're doctors," says the woman.

"They infect us with diseases and then experiment with medicine," the man says. "There were others here before but we're the last ones left."

"There's these creatures," the woman says, and starts crying. "Please..."

"It's time," Jonas says.

"My god," Amos says, now dazed in some kind of shock.

"Let's go," Quinn says.

Jonas pushes the button to turn off the studio audio and grabs Amos by the collar and says, "It's time!" Steering him away from the control panel and towards the door.

"They're already here," the voice says.

And just then, the door opens up and two armed guards rush in aiming pistols at the four of you. "Freeze right there!" one of them yells.

"Gentlemen, stand down," Jonas says, hands up and slowly moving towards them. "We got a call here to repair the ventilation system, real serious stuff, it's not safe for you–"

"Stop right there!" says the other guard.

"Gentlemen, it's ok," Jonas says, still moving towards them. "We're here to help." Suddenly, he lunges for the guard closest to him and grabs the pistol forcing the guard to aim up. A shot is fired! Amos runs into the melee, and another shot is fired. Then another and another shot! Now, it's just one of the guards with his arm around Amos holding him at gunpoint. Jonas and the other guard are both motionless on the ground next to a pistol. Amos kicks the pistol towards you and it slides to a stop at your feet.

"Nobody fucking move!" the guard says. "I don't want anyone else to get hurt."

You look at Quinn and she looks back at you in shock.

The belly of her white jumpsuit is bright red. She looks down at her stomach and clutches it with both hands.

"Amos," she whispers.

"I'm so sorry," Amos says to Quinn.

You look back at Amos.

"Do it," he says.

"Kill them both," the voice says.

"Get on the ground right now!" the guard says.

In what feels like a moment of frozen time, you look at the man and woman in the studio prison who are watching, cowered in the corner. You look at the reptilian humanoid whose face is practically pressed against the glass as it stares at you.

Suddenly, Amos fights to break free from the guard, but in the scuffle the guard shoots Amos who collapses to the ground.

This may be your only chance to survive, one way or the other. Grab the gun at your feet and shoot to kill. Or do as the guard says and surrender.

Surrender and hope for the best, turn to page 95.
Grab the pistol and shoot the guard, turn to page 101.

This is their show, not yours. You wait. Shouldn't they be the ones to come ashore and make themselves clearly known and visible. Right now, they're just hiding in the boat in the shadows. Something doesn't feel right.

You decide to give it a few minutes and see what they do. If they start the outboard motor again to leave, you'll come out.

Suddenly, you can hear another engine approaching. This one is much larger. And then you see it: a black van speeding towards you on the park pathway along the river. The men in the boat see it too and are now trying to start the boat's motor. But it's too late.

The van careens up the path to a screeching halt between you and the boat, blocking your view. You can see some men get out of the van and then a gunshot! You crouch lower to ensure you can't be seen but every cell in your body screams to run.

You can hear the men talking but can't quite make out what they're saying. There's some splashing in the water. You watch as two men from the van forcibly walk the man from the boat around the front of the van. Another man opens the sliding side door of the van and motions for the man from the boat to get in. He nods and feigns like he's getting in but then takes off running. His footsteps ring out on the pathway as one of the men from the van calmly pulls out his gun and shoots the fleeing man twice in the back.

You audibly gasp, almost shriek. And both the driver and passenger are now looking in your direction. They heard you. And now they're running towards you!

You bolt, you don't even think about it, you just take off running.

You can hear them running behind you and yelling: "Stop! Stop right there!"

You keep running, running as hard as you can, but you misstep off the pathway curb and fall face-first onto the asphalt. You're blinded by the fall and struggle to get back to your feet. And as soon as you do, you're tackled hard by one of the men and pinned to the ground. Before you can even try to fight back, your hands are zip tied behind your back.

The man rolls you over onto your back and stands up. You can barely see through the blood pouring into your eyes.

"I'll be damned," says one of the men. "It's him."

The other man laughs.

"Stick him and get him in the van," the one man says. "Let's get out of here."

The other man kneels down next do you and you feel a sharp prick in your neck as everything fades to black.

Continue, turn to page 77.

What in the hell do you think you're doing? You can't go through with this. Get out of there!

You lock the door, pocket the key and make your way around the house to the back, across the yard and back into your parents' house. You put the key away and remove your gloves, hat, and mask.

You feel relieved but also you're shaking from the adrenaline. This is the right thing to do, you tell yourself. You're not a criminal. You're mad, you're upset, and you should be, but making that call would've been wrong. That's not the way.

Not really sure what to do with yourself now, you decide to take a shower. At least there you can be sure to be alone, not that your parents noticed that you stepped out for a moment.

In the shower, letting the hot water pelt your face as the bathroom gets foggy with steam, you begin to relax only by realizing how tense you were: your shoulders, your jaw, your throat, all your muscles begin to loosen. You breathe deeply, feeling like you almost made a terrible mistake. But you didn't. You did the right thing.

You finish your shower and get dressed with a lightness you haven't felt in quite some time. Heading to the kitchen to make some breakfast you pass by the living room where your parents stand staring at the television.

"What's going on?" you ask.

"A bomb went off downtown," your dad says. "And looks like a few other places too."

"What?" you say, looking at the television: images of the Multnomah County Detention Center on fire with its facade completely gutted. The ticker at the bottom of the screen reads: HUNDREDS DEAD IN DOWNTOWN BOMBING.

"Who would do such a thing?" your mother asks with tears streaming down her face.

"It was real," you say, without realizing you're speaking out loud.

The newscast is interrupted by a desk anchor who says, "We're now going live to Seattle where we've received news of two nearly simultaneous explosions."

"Seattle too?" your dad says.

"What do you mean?" you ask.

"Downtown, Portland East, Beaverton, Salem, two places in California, and now Seattle," your dad says. "It seems like a coordinated terrorist attack."

The desk anchor continues, saying, "We're receiving reports indicating that in advance of many but not all of these attacks anonymous callers were phoned in to warn those inside about the bombs. With these advance notices many of the buildings were evacuated before the explosions."

You crumple to the carpeted floor of your parents' living room. You can't breathe. You feel like you're screaming but nothing is coming out and everything is silent.

"Honey, are you ok?" your mother asks.

Those militants lied to you, yes. But you will never be able to shake the guilt of being responsible, fully aware or not, for those deaths. You could've saved them. You could've saved them with a phone call.

If only you had gone through with the plan.

You've survived 2020, but many others have not.

THE END

"This wasn't the plan," you say. "I can't go through with this."

"We're past the point of return," Quinn says. "You don't have much of a choice. Remember Reno."

"Fuck you," you say. "I'm out of here." You exit the van and head towards the gate through which you entered.

"Code ten!" Quinn yells at the twins.

You look back and see Jonas running at you full speed. You take off running but he catches up to you almost immediately and tackles you to the ground. You struggle to fight him off and he rolls you over onto your belly and you feel a pinch on your butt. Jonas gets off of you and stands. You roll over and try to sit up but for some reason you can't. Your body feels very heavy and your movements are slow.

"Dammit," Amos says now standing over you with Jonas. "We keep moving, stick with the plan.. Who cares what happens to the scapegoat."

Your vision blurs, then goes black as you lose consciousness.

When you awake, you find yourself on the floor in a strange metal room with one wall of frosted, opaque glass. Quinn is there too, sitting on one of the two beds.

"What happened?" you ask while sitting up. Dizzy, you lean against the wall. "Where are we?"

"We failed," Quinn says, staring off into space. "We failed."

Suddenly the door to the room opens and three large men in full hazmat suits enter. They approach Quinn. And without speaking they grab her and lift her off her feet as she screams and tries to fight.

"Hey!" you say. "What're you doing?"

Quinn continues to scream as the three men carry her out of the room and close the door.

Silence. You're alone.

"What the hell is going on here!" you scream. "Where am I?"

The door opens again and in walk three men in hazmat suits. They pause, standing there in silencee.

"Stay away from me!" you say. "Stay back!"

Then they approach you. You stand but they grab you by the shoulders and sit you back down, holding you there.

You stuggle and break free but you're tackled.

The men pin you down to the ground. Despite fighting with all your strength, you cannot escape their grasp. A fourth man in a hazmat suit enters the room and approaches you. He's holding a large syringe.

"Stay still," he says through his respirator.

"What the hell is that?" you scream as he injects your arm with the contents of the syringe. "What the hell is that!"

The fourth man leaves, followed by the other three and now you're alone again in silence on the floor of this room.

"Hey!" you scream. "Someone tell me what the hell is going on here! Hello!"

With a sudden click, the glass wall goes clear and you can see through the window into a larger control room of sorts with a team of men and women in white lab coats. One of them sits at a desk facing your room.

He speaks into a microphone and you hear him through speakers in your room: "How are you feeling?"

"How am I feeling!" you say. "Who the hell are you?"

"Answer the questions," he says. "How are you feeling?"

"I feel pretty pissed off!" you say. "I feel–" suddenly, your stomach seizes in pain and you double over. Your whole body begins to cramp and stiffen.

"How are you feeling?"

You fall to your hands and knees in pain, screaming. It feels as if the blood in your veins is on fire. You suddenly vomit. It's red.

"How are you feeling?"

You collapse, losing consciousness. Lying there face-down in your own bloody vomit, your heart stops.

The men and women wearing lab coats in the control room sigh collectively. One of them pats the interrogator on the shoulder, consolingly.

Another man in a lab coat says, "Get the room reset, we'll

try with the other one now.."

You are just another victim of whatever experiments these people are conducting, whatever contagions or compounds they're injecting into those they've captured or kidnapped.

You did not survive 2020.

And the experiments continue...

THE END

You awake startled and scared. You had a terrible nightmare of people attacking you in your bed. And then you realize: you're not in your bed.

You're on a cot in a small, windowless room. You sit up and quickly scan the room: there's a door, plain gray walls, a surveillance camera mounted high in the corner but otherwise there's nothing in the room. It's a cell.

You're dizzy, sat up too fast. And the vivid details of your "dream" return to you: the men who attacked you were real, and they drugged you. You rub your neck and can feel the puncture wound from the needle. What the hell is happening?

You stand up slowly. You carefully walk to the door and try the handle. It's locked. You look back at the camera.

This can't really be happening. This can't really be happening.

Suddenly the door opens and in walks an older man, in his 60s, wearing a gray suit. "Please, have a seat," he says, with a Russian accent. He motions to the bed.

You sit, still in a weird state of disbelief and shock.

"My name is Charles," the man says. "This is going to be a bit surprising to hear – what I'm about to tell you – but it's important that you believe me. You need to trust me, ok?"

"Who are you?"

"I'm Charles."

"Yeah, but who the hell are you?" you say. "Where am I? What is going on here?"

"Listen," he says. "Please, it's important that you listen very closely. Pay attention to what I'm about to say to you." Charles sighs again, and loosens his tie while glancing at the surveillance camera. He looks back at you and says, "I'm your only friend here. And if you want any chance at making it through all of this, you'll need to trust me, ok? Can you try to do that? Can you trust me?"

It doesn't feel like you have much of a choice.

"What choice do you have really?" Charles says.

"What?" you yelp. Did he just read your mind?

"I work for a very powerful organization that has governed this world for a very long time. And we need your help."

"So you kidnap me?"

"Yes," Charles said, plainly. "It could've been worse. And it can still get worse. But if you cooperate with us, you'll do just fine."

"But you kidnapped me!"

"That doesn't matter. What matters is you're here now, and you're alive, and we're going to keep you alive. We're going to protect you. But there are two ways we can do this. You can be cooperative and remain... comfortable. Or you can not corporate, and this will be very, very unpleasant for you."

"What do you want me to do? Where am I?"

"You're currently in an underground base in Antarctica."

"No."

"Yes," Charles says. "You're in the safest place on the planet right now. The Coronavirus? In the next few years, we anticipate it will kill half the population on the planet, around four billion people. There's no cure. There will never be a cure. No vaccine, no protection, no safety. And the rest of the population, well, some will suffer fates worse than death: starvation, anarchy, riots, storms, fires... Earth is very mad, and nothing will stop her vengeance."

Charles pulls out a pack of cigarettes, and offers one to you. You shake your head. He shrugs, and lights one for himself.

"I want to go home," you say.

"Keep it together, ok?" Charles says, taking a pull from his cigarette. "I'm going to take you into the next room and show you some things that you may not want to believe but you have to trust me and keep it together, ok?"

You swallow hard.

"Ok," you say.

"Ok" Charles says. "Good. But first, here's what you need to know: there is a very, very, very small percentage of humans who have immunity to COVD-19. And you're one of them."

"What? How do you know?"

"We know," Charles says. "And we've discovered that

through blood transfusions, dialysis, plasma, CRISPR technology... we can actually help save people from COVID with the help of those with immunity."

Charles sucks from his cigarette, which is slowly filling the small room with smoke.

"Look," he says. "You're going to help us whether you want to or not. The only thing that's up to you is..."

Suddenly, the door opens and standing in the doorway is a large man, but it's not a man. It's a reptilian humanoid: a man, wearing pants and a shirt, with the head of a reptile, not quite snake or alligator or lizard but something like all three combined.

"Goddammit," Charles says. "We're not ready."

"What the hell?" you yelp.

"He's ready," the reptilian humanoid says, though he doesn't move his mouth. "Bring him." The creature turns and walks away.

Charles takes a drag of his cigarette and exhales slowly, looking at you. "It's not a conspiracy theory," he says. "Try to remain calm, ok? Let's go."

Charles walks out of the room and you slowly follow into a massive facility that looks part hospital and part NASA control center. Dozens of men and reptilian humanoids operate desk stations with touchscreen computer monitors. Most men are wearing light blue jumpsuits but some are wearing lab coats. The reptilian humanoids are wearing suit pants and white shirts, though some wear no shirt at all, just bare green, muscular, scaly torsos.

There's a low level of commotion as some move from station to station, examining information, sharing devices, whispering and chatting among themselves. Strangest of all, no one seems to even notice you standing there in your pajamas next to Charles still smoking.

"This way," he says, taking a drag of his cigarette. "I want to show you something."

You follow Charles to one of the computer stations where a man is sitting. The man goes to stand but Charles puts his hand on his shoulder to sit him back down. "Show us

'Immunity Group 14'," Charles orders.

"Yes, sir," the man says and types in some keystroke command and the large monitor shows a grid of nine video feeds from what appears to be nine different rooms.

Each room, of varying sizes, is nicely furnished and looks like a modern studio apartment you'd find in any large city. Some rooms have one or two people and some rooms have three or four people. You notice in one room a young man and woman having sex. Another room shows another couple cooking dinner and the woman looks nine months pregnant. Another room shows four women chatting and sharing a bottle of wine. Another room shows a man alone playing video games.

"You see," Charles says. "We want you to be happy. We want you to be comfortable, build relationships, have children, enjoy yourselves." He takes a long drag of his cigarette and watches you watch the screens, making sure you see what he wants you to see. "But it's up to you, of course."

Charles taps the station controller's shoulder and orders him to switch to "Immunity Group 7."

The grid of video feeds flickers and changes to one large video feed of a single room, what looks like a hospital room lined with beds, each with a sleeping patient. There were at least seven or eight but looks like there could be more hidden off camera. Every patient has an IV and a number of monitors. And every single one of them is asleep.

"It's pretty straightforward," Charles says. "If you don't cooperate with us we put you in a medically induced coma and take what we need anyway. I'm sure we can count on your cooperation."

You look at Charles and he's giving you a face as if to say, "Don't be stupid, kid."

You nod, looking down.

Suddenly, there's gunfire and screaming! You duck behind the computer console. There's more shooting and now yelling: "Drop it!" then "You drop it!"

"Don't shoot!" someone orders. You look up and it's Charles, now standing in the middle of the room with his hands in the air. "Put your weapons down," he says.

You can see a small group of armed security officers pointing their guns at a couple of people hiding among the computer stations.

"I said holster your weapons, dammit!" Charles yells.

The security team reluctantly holsters their pistols.

"Now," Charles says. "Henry, is that you?"

"Fuck you, Charles!" someone yells back.

"Henry," Charles says. "No need to hide, no one is going to hurt you."

"Yeah, maybe I hurt you!" Henry says, leaping up and aiming his pistol at Charles. Crouching behind Henry is a blond woman also pointing her pistol at Charles. She's pregnant.

You lean further around your console to see the bodies of a technician and two security officers on the ground in pools of blood.

"Henry, please," Charles says. "Don't do this, we can work it out."

"We're leaving, Charles," Henry says. "We're not going to be your guinea pigs any more!"

You make eye contact with Henry.

"That your new test subject?" Henry asks Charles. "Do you have any idea what they do to people here?" he screams at you. "Do you have any idea who these monsters really are?"

Charles looks at you somberly and motions with palm down for you to stay put.

"Come with us," Henry says to you. "This is your only chance."

"Where do you think you're going to go?" Charles asks. "There's nowhere to go."

"I have a plan, Charles, don't you worry about us," Henry says. "Last chance," he says to you and kicks the gun of one of the dead security officers across the floor. It spins while sliding toward you leaving a streak of blood in its wake. It slowly comes to a stop just in front of you.

"You'll never make it," Charles says.

"Oh yes we will," Henry says.

You can pick up the pistol and join in Henry's escape

plan, or do nothing and stay out of trouble.

If you're really in Antarctica, how are you going to get to safety? Then again, if this is truly your one and only chance to escape, taking the chance may be worth it.

Faced with the life of a guinea pig for Russian sociopaths and reptilian humanoids, you may want to risk freezing to death.

Neither option is great, but it's time to make a decision.

Grab the gun and try to escape, turn to page 86.
Do nothing and stay out of trouble, turn to page 94.

Enough is enough. You're staying in D.C., and making your voice heard. No justice, no peace!

The next day the band members who chose to stay, including Chloe, Beau, and yourself, take to the streets but leave the musical instruments at home. Having connected with local leadership and formed a cohesive plan, you feel prepared and empowered. And the streets are now full of demonstrators.

It is Friday, May 29th, 2020.

By sundown you find yourself with hundreds of other protestors at Lafayette Square near the White House. Word spreads quickly through the crowd that the White House is on lock down and the President is hiding in an underground bunker. Despite some small incidents with the Secret Service, the gathering is peaceful, joyful even. It feels really good to be a part of something, to have your voice heard, to know that they're scared of you.

The next day, you take part in more of the same: marching and protesting during the day with small skirmishes at night between demonstrators and police. You hear of police cars being set on fire and graffiti at the National Mall. Whose streets? Our streets!

The next day you march with even more people heading straight down 15th Street along the East Wing of the White House. You hear of police attacking reporters and looting in Georgetown, and Farragut Square.

In the morning, you wake up to the news that Mayor Bowser announced a citywide curfew beginning at 7pm. That day there were more protestors than ever! You march all day long, singing songs, chanting, saying their names: George Floyd, Breonna Taylor, Eric Garner, Trayvon Martin, Sean Bell, Freddie Gray, Sandra Bland, and others.

That evening, you and Chloe and Beau make your way to Lafayette Square, the park neighboring the White House. It's beautiful, full of passionate, empathetic, people. Yes, they're angry and upset, but this is how we make our voices heard.

The crowd is thick. It's less of a march now and more of a gathering. There's press and camera crews, medics and supply teams, people holding cardboard signs, and people wearing gas masks and goggles.

"It's after six," Beau says.

"Fuck the curfew," Chloe says.

Suddenly, a loud commotion sounds from the crowd. People are screaming. The cops and National Guard have attacked! One minute everything is peaceful and calm and now it's chaos, bedlam. Tear gas wafts through the air and you can see riot police beating a woman with their batons. You grab Chloe and run the other direction as tear gas canisters fly over your head landing in front of you and rolling along the street emitting thick, white smoke. Explosions! It's a warzone. You make your way north through teh crowd.

Retreating up 16th Street, you and Chloe and Beau take a moment to rest and regroup. Chloe is suffering, her eyes burn and her throat hurts. You decide to head to the house.

Back home, while Chloe showers you and Beau make dinner. Scrolling the news feeds, you learn that Trump and his lackeys had ordered the police and National Guard to attack the protestors and clear the area so that he could pose for photos in front of St. John's Episcopal Church.

"It was a fucking photo op," Beau says.

Troops and police had used tear gas, rubber bullets, pepper spray, and stingball grenades to clear the protestors. Then they pursued the crowd of protestors on horses, and riot police continued to push back the demonstrators.

"A fucking photo op," Beau says, loudly plating the pasta dinner for the three of you.

While you eat, the other band members return to the house with a few new people. Together, they vow to take action and take it to the next level. "It's time to fight fire with fire," someone says.

These new people seem a bit more radical, a bit more committed to the cause.

"They come for us," someone says. "We're gonna come for them."

They have a plan. And everyone is involved, ready for action. This seems serious.

"This is serious," someone says. "Anyone who is not

down for the cause needs to either get down with the cause or get lost. We ain't messing around here, this is war."

Who are these new people? All of a sudden everyone is very pissed off and very serious. Are you on board? Maybe it's too much after what went down today.

Are you ready for a real fight?

If this is just a bit too much, turn to page 97.
If you're on board, turn to page 108.

Fight or flight, right? Well, this is both.

You pick up the bloody pistol and cautiously, slowly walk towards Henry and the blonde woman. Your eyes move from Charles to Henry to the security team, and back to Charles.

"You're making a mistake," Charles says.

You find yourself now standing next to Henry. You slowly raise your arm to point your gun at Charles.

"A big mistake," Charles says.

"Shut up," Henry says. "We're moving, let's go."

And the three of you walk across the room towards one of the larger, double doors. Everyone watches you as you step one foot at a time with guns aimed at Charles. At the door, Henry enters a code on a keypad and the doors open.

"Don't do it," Charles says.

You step through the doorway, the door closes behind you, and Henry and the blonde take off running down the brightly lit corridor. You chase after them. It seems there's no end in sight, and for some reason it feels like you're running uphill.

You pass an intersecting corridor but Henry and the blonde keep running straight. "Come on!" Henry says. "We're almost there!"

You can now see the end of the corridor: a large, red door.

"We gotta move quickly once we're outside," Henry says. "There's a Sno-Cat maybe twenty yards away, so just head straight for that as fast as you can."

The three of you reach the red door and take just a moment to catch your breath. The door is metal with a large handle, like a door on a submarine.

"A snow cat?" you ask.

"A Sno-Cat," Henry says, exasperated. "A truck, a tank, a big damn truck, ok?"

Henry and the blonde look at each other and kiss.

Looking back the way you came you can see two groups of soldiers on an electric carts driving towards you.

Henry turns the handle and the door opens inward with a flurry of freezing wind and snow.

Outside is only white. You can't see a horizon, only snow.

Henry and the blonde run out and you follow, but soon enough you realize there's a problem.

"Where is it?" the blonde cries.

"It should be here!" Henry screams.

The wind is loud and snow is pelting your face. You can't see anything. You're almost knee-deep in snow.

Henry looks panicked, looking all around him, practically spinning in circles, searching for a truck that isn't there.

"What do we do?" the blonde wails.

"We go back," Henry says. "We'll die if we stay out here, we have to go back."

So you three start running back to the doorway, open and bright with the light of the corridor. But as you get closer, the light goes dim. And you can see Charles now standing in the doorway.

"No!" Henry yells.

You're all running as fast as you can, but you don't make it to the corridor before Charles closes the door with a loud thud and a clank of the handle locking.

Henry bangs his fist against the door, screaming, not really saying anything, just screaming. The blonde holds her rounded stomach as the wind and snow whip through her hair.

Somehow you're calm, confident that you know at least one real and true thing about this crazy world: this is where you're going to die.

Henry continues to scream.

The blonde looks at you with icy eyebrows and rosy cheeks and says, "I'm sorry."

You did not survive 2020.

THE END

"Ok," you say, dismounting your bike and propping it against a streetlight pole. You walk around the van and climb in through the side door joining three others. They are not happy to see you.

The leader climbs in the driver's seat, closes the door, starts the engine, and drives. She makes the first right turn, and takes the on-ramp to enter Interstate 405 heading south and then Interstate 84 heading east.

No one speaks as you drive for hours and hours. Exciting the freeway you head down a winding state route road deep into a forest for another hour, then onto a smaller road, then an even smaller road, then a dirt road and finally the horizon reveals a meadow with a few buildings, a house and barns, and the van stops.

After a few moments, you see a grey van driving towards you from behind one of the barns. The van pulls up directly beside your van and without speaking everyone from your van takes all their belongings and moves from the purple van into the grey van and you follow.

Now in the grey van, you continue your drive east, across the Snake River and into Idaho.

Eventually, you seem to have reached your destination: a secluded hamlet of just a few homes and barns on a hilltop surrounded by farmland: green, rolling hills as far as you can see. The five of you in the van exit and walk slowly up the hill towards the houses where a few men and women come out to greet you.

Without much talk, you're invited into the house where they've prepared a meal for everyone and you dine without conversation while the sun sets outside. When everyone's finished eating, one of the men from the house says, "Let's join the rest at the fire," before standing and leaving.

Slowly, everyone follows outside to discover a very large bonfire, with flames over 10 feet tall. There are about two dozen people around the fire gathered in small groups, talking, laughing, some sitting, some standing.

With very little fanfare at all, you and your group are welcomed close to the fire and then many of the people stop their conversations and watch you patiently. First, the leader of your group takes out her wallet and throws it all into the fire. Then another man in your group tosses his wallet into the fire. And then the other two throw their wallets in the fire.

You take out your wallet and look inside: a few single dollar bills, your driver's license, health insurance card, an old MetroCard from what feels like an eternity ago... the leader of your group puts her hand on your shoulder, supportive but also persuasive.

You toss your wallet into the fire.

"Welcome," says the man who led you to the bonfire. He gives you a hug as the others shake hands and embrace in the bright orange glow of the fire.

You've survived 2020, but at what cost?

THE END

You don't need to rush out to Central Park in the middle of the night with UFOs showing up all over the place. People are out there losing their minds, looting, doing who knows what.

The Russian press briefing is happening soon. Let's see how that goes down before we go rushing out to meet the aliens, or whatever they are.

CNN now has a live map of the world with the positions of all 57 UFOs hovering silently over cities all around the world. Somewhat surprisingly, it seems that no government or military has attempted an attack on the crafts. Though, it's only been a couple of hours since they appeared.

Scientists and physicists alike are completely perplexed by the crafts, which emit no sound, no air disturbance, no motion whatsoever. They appeared suddenly, simultaneously. It's not yet known where they came from or how they arrived.

News reports say that the UN has called for an emergency video meeting and while most citizens around the world have kept from catastrophic, violent panic, the world's markets are collapsing in real time with the Shanghai Composite, the Hang Seng, and the Nikkei in Japan all reporting unprecedented losses.

Is this how the world comes to an end?

Breaking news! "We're now going live from Moscow," the news anchor says. "As Russian leadership reportedly meets with the exterrestrials from the craft." The video cuts to a large stage built in Red Square with the colorful Saint Basil's Cathedral as a background. A large crowd has gathered, though there is a large, open space with security guards between the public and a small press pit at the base of the stage. "We're told that the extraterrestrials are currently in talks with Russian leadership," the news anchor says. "Though with whom exactly, we're not sure. Wait – something seems to be happening, there is some movement among the people on stage and, yes, we have something now. Here come representatives of Russia stepping up onto the stage, and… my god…"

There, on live video, Russian leaders step onto a stage in Red Square with four tall, slender grey aliens following behind them. At least 10-feet tall, they tower over the humans around them, and while seemingly naked and without clothes, they do not appear to have any genitalia, and each looks almost identical: long limbs, long fingers, big round and flat heads with large, black, almond-shaped eyes.

A Russian diplomat steps to the microphone stand and speaks to the crowd, saying, translated into English on the video: "Today is a miraculous and historic day. Not just for our country, but for the world. Today we finally have the answer to the question we've been asking since the dawn of humanity: we are not alone."

The Russiasn crowd applauds languidly, perhaps still in shock. From the rooftop of your building you hear a commotion. Maybe people are up there watching this as well? But then it grows louder, people yelling and screaming at each other, you hear people clamouring through the hallway.

"As Russians," the ambassador says, continuing his speech. "We welcome our new comrades…"

The hallway commotion is louder now. It sounds like people are fighting? You approach your apartment door cautiously, and open it slowly. In the hallway you see a few people racing down the stairs. Everything is blue. Shining through the roof hatch is a pale blue light so bright that seems to paint the floor and walls.

You can't help but be drawn to the light. Stepping forward you enter the hallway and gaze up through the hatch into the light but can see nothing beyond a shimmering blue, as if looking at the sun from under the surface of the ocean. Slowly, carefully, without thought or concern, you climb the ladder up to the roof. Emerging through the roof hatch you're bathed in the shimmering pale blue light. Though blinded, you have no fear.

The light feels like more than light. You're floating in it, something like swimming in it. The air is not air. Then, there's nothing.

Now you're seated in a large otherwise empty room with no windows. The ceiling is so high as to be out of sight. You're breathing, blinking, looking around, but otherwise you cannot move. You cannot stand from the chair. And then you see something moving in the distant shadows.

One of the grey aliens approaches you. It moves slowly, like a heavy giant, but steps lightly almost as if its feet do not touch the ground. It comes to stand before you and towers over you with it's long, thin arms by its sides. In its large, black eyes you see your refleciton.

It speaks without sound: "We have been watching you. You are a chosen one. Now you too have a choice. You may accept our offering and ascend to a level of knowledge and awareness your species does not understand. Or you may decline and return to your world as you were, as others before you have also chosen. There is no right or wrong decision. In each, there is pain. In each, there is joy. And by choosing one you will sacrifice the other. I can tell you no more. Now... what is your choice?"

Accept the alien's offer, turn to page 115.
Decline the alien's offer, turn to page 161.

You've come this far. Nothing this man is going to say to you is going to change anything: you either trust him or you don't.

"Okay," you say, wading into the river. When you reach the boat and see this man eye-to-eye you find that he's much younger than he seemed. He's handsome, and fit, and seems somehow trustworthy. He takes your arm and helps you step into the boat.

"Welcome aboard," says the other man, a bit older, helming the outboard motor. "Have a seat." And he yanks hard on the pull cord and starts the engine.

You sit as the boat lurches forward into the river. The man with the cap is also sitting, facing you, and he's holding something in his hand.

Suddenly, you feel a sharp pain in your chest. Looking down, you see a metal dart with a red feathered end sticking out of your chest.

"Don't worry," says the man with the cap. "It's just a mild sedative until we can get you to the next boat."

"What?" You ask.

"You'll be fine," the man with the cap says, as you slowly lose consciousness while he gently lays you down in the boat. "You'll be juuuuuuuuuust fiiiiiiiiiinnnnnnnnnnnne."

Continue, turn to page 102.

Something doesn't seem right.

Well, that's an understatement, but something about these two with guns trying to flee just doesn't add up. What if we actually are in Antarctica?

You kick the gun and it slides across the floor back toward Henry and the blonde.

Immediately, they take off running out the room into what looks like a long hallway.

"You chose wisely," Charles says, putting his hand on your shoulder. "Now, come with me."

"What about them?" you ask.

"What about them?" Charles replies, steering you around the security officer bodies and pools of blood.

"Aren't you going to go after them?"

"They're not going anywhere," Charles says.

"What do you mean?" you ask. You're now both standing before a door with a keypad.

Charles pauses and sighs. "If they manage to get outside, they'll freeze to death in minutes. And inside, they'll either go down shooting or they'll surrender. Those are their options. I'm not going after them, because there's nowhere for them to go."

He looks almost sad explaining this to you. As if he's a prisoner himself.

"Now," he says, forcing himself to perk up. "Let's go see your new room, shall we?" He punches a code into the keypad and the door opens. "After you," he says.

You enter, crossing the threshold into your new life as a well-kept Russian prisoner and human guinea pig for reptilian humanoid scientists in a secret, underground facility deep underground in Antarctica.

Congratulations, you've survived 2020.

THE END

"Ok," you say, raising your hands high in the air. "Don't shoot. I'm going to get down on the ground now."

"Don't move!" the guard screams at you.

You freeze and remain silent.

The door to the outside opens and someone says from outside: "This is Navy Yard security, do not shoot."

The guard calls back, saying, "I'm here, I have them!"

In walks a tall, skinny man in a black suit. He's older, weathered, with deep age lines in his leathery face. "You did well, son," he says to the guard.

"Thank you, sir," the guard says, shaking a bit, still aiming the gun at you.

The tall, skinny man steps towards the security guard, pulls out a handgun, and shoots the guard in the head. The guard drops to the floor.

The tall, skinny man takes a few steps to stand over Amos's body and fires one shot down into Amos's head. Then he walks to stand over the other guard and fires into his head and again fires into Jonas's head. He then walks over to Quinn's body and fires to put a bullet in her head.

Finally, the tall, skinny man approaches you. "Did the creature speak to you?" he asks.

You look at the reptilian humanoid who stares back at you in silence. Yes, you heard the voice, the creature's telepathic communication. But should you admit that?

"What did it say?" asks the tall, skinny man. "What did you hear?"

Play dumb, turn to page 107.
Tell the truth, turn to page 120.

"Screw you," you say. "You're crazy. You're murderers! Terrorists!"

The leader says nothing and just simply climbs in the van and drives away, leaving you standing in the road straddling your bike as police car sirens blair in the distance.

Not knowing what else to do, you ride slowly through downtown and eventually back towards your parents house. Turning onto your street, you see a number of police cars in front of your house.

You stop short but it's too late. Two of the police officers standing in your parents driveway have spotted you. "Hey!" one shouts.

"Stop right there," another one shouts.

The first cop pulls out his gun and aims at you. "I said freeze!"

The other officer is now also pointing his gun at you as they both move towards you.

"Dismount the bike," one says. "Get off the bike and get on the ground right now!"

"OK," you say, moving very slowly.

"It was you wasn't it?" someone screams. You look over to see your neighbor George, the MCDC corrections officer. He's walking briskly across his front lawn towards you. "You set off that bomb, didn't you!" Is he holding something?

"No," you say. "I'm sor–"

"Oh just shut up," George says, raising his arm, pointing his pistol, and shooting you five times in the chest.

You did not survive 2020.

THE END

"I'm just gonna head to the roof for a bit," you tell Beau.

"Aight," Beau says.

Alone on the roof, you feel at peace. Like everything you've seen and done this week is settling within you, becoming a part of you. This week in D.C. has changed your life.

And for now, it's nice to be alone, on the roof, under the stars... That's strange, those stars are moving.

Oh my god, those are not stars. They're spacecraft. You watch as maybe a dozen UFOs descend upon the city stopping to hover above buildings. Police sirens sound down from the street.

In the distance, you can see three UFOs directly above the Capitol Building.

Now Beau is on the roof with you. "What the hell is going on?" he asks.

"I have no idea," you say.

And you both watch as the bottom of the UFOs open up to reveal a bright, blue light that then descends like falling water in a tube. Are they beaming down or beaming something up?

Either way, you feel a strange sense of relief. Perhaps it's gratitude? The arrival of extraterrestrials may actually fix this mess, or at least help bring us together, as a planet, as humans, as one...

Then again, the aliens may be here to destroy us. We'll find out soon enough.

Congratulations, you've survived 2020... for now!

THE END

There's no way you're going to sit in your bedroom while there are UFOs above Central Park. You pack a small bag with some water and snacks, and head out. It's pretty quiet in your neighborhood and you slowly make your way to the Brooklyn Bridge where, for two in the morning, it's surprisingly crowded. You're not the only one who's heading to the UFOs. Everyone is excited, happy, and wide eyed. There are more than a few zealots, going on and on about the end of the world, repenting, that sort of thing. But for the most part it's a nice scene.

Once you get over the bridge into lower Manhattan though, everything changes. It seems like there isn't a single police officer in the city, as people loot without concern or consequence. You pass one storefront on fire, then another one. It feels like there are two worlds occuring simultaneously and neither world has any care or concern for the other one. The pilgrims are merely passing through and the looters care not, each group with its own mission.

Walking through Washington Square Park the entire fountain area is packed: Musicians play, priests lead prayer, vendors sell inflatable green alien balloons like they were somehow prepared for this event.

There's a small group of you now, walking together, an unspoken collective as you pass through areas of retail and looting and large gatherings in parks. Union Square has a massive crowd that feels like a full-on black party. The Stereo Exchange and Paragon Sports both are broken and emptied. Madison Square Park has a relatively small crowd. Walgreens, Sephora, Victoria's Secret, Urban Outfitters, all of the stores near Penn Station have been ransacked.

You reach Bryant Park and realize that, yes, the city still has a police force and it seems that every single one of them is here. It appears as if they've drawn a line in the sand and that line is 40th Street.

You look at your quiet companions and one says to the group, "We should be able to go around them at some point?" You nod and your group heads west along 40th street. Each intersection is blocked and patrolled by dozens of police, armored vehicles, and spotlights.

Then, you reach 9th Avenue and discover the police have set up a checkpoint there, allowing anyone uptown to evacuate south along 9th Avenue and only 9th Avenue. It's a mess.

Police are screaming at people, cars are honking, this is your chance. You duck down and make your way into the street, moving between cars, heading uptown against the traffic. You make it through and imagine that even if the police saw you, they didn't care enough to stop you. But now you're on your own.

Midtown is a very different scene, desolate and silent. You make your way up 8th Avenue and reach Columbus Circle, where you now have your first up close view of the UFOs. One is directly above you, enormous, blocking out the entire sky and completely, inexplicably still.

The craft's underbelly looks like metal but has a wavy shimmer like water. Dim lights seem to randomly illuminate and then darken at various spots on the craft. It's a bizarre sensation, looking up and not seeing the sky.

"Hey," a man says. There's a policeman standing not far from you. "How'd you get up here?"

You start walking backwards, away from him.

"Wait," he says. "I'm not really a cop."

Your instinct is to bolt, make a run for it.

"That's how I got in," he says. "I dressed like a cop, had this costume from last Halloween."

Something's not right, you think. This is weird, getting weirder. You look towards the entrance of the park.

"Don't go that way," he says. "They'll catch you. We have to go around, I'll show you."

Do you trust this man? Even if he's not a real cop, why would he want to help you? You're made it this far on your own. Then again, he may know what he's talking about.

Trust him and follow his lead, turn to page 111.
Run into the park, turn to page 118.

"Listen," you say. "This is all just a bit much for me... the letter, whoever the hell you are, now this boat... I just need you to tell me what exactly is going on here."

The man removes his cap and rubs his forearm across his forehead and then puts his cap back on. "I get it," he says. "The truth is... that's just not really an option at the moment."

"What?"

The man then pulls out a gun and shots you in the chest. It hurts but for some reason you're still standing. You look down and see the red feathery end of a tranquilizer dart sticking out of your chest.

"You've got about ten seconds before you're lights out," he says. "Do us both a favor and get in the boat so you don't drown in shallow water?"

"You shot me," you say, and the sound of your own voice is warbly and dissonant.

"He's gonna drop," says the man in the boat.

"I got him," says the man in the cap who is now taking you on his shoulder into the water and folding you into the boat.

As you lose consciousness, the last thing you hear is the man in the cap telling you: "It's going to be ok, it's all going to be ok."

Continue, turn to page 102.

You quickly crouch down, pick up the pistol, aim, and fire… you keep firing until the gun stops. The guard is dead. You look to Quinn who is now quivering on the floor.

Without thinking too much, you move quickly and find the two GoPro cameras on the floor. Jonas, Amos, and Quinn lie still and lifeless. The guards on the floor are also dead. You put the cameras in your jumpsuit pocket.

The two humans in their studio cell stand at the glass. They're in shock, mesmerized. You see them staring at you. The lizard creature? It seems even larger than it was, its shoulders, its neck, its head, as it presses its face and hands against the glass watching you.

"I'm your only hope," you hear the voice say. "Your mission will fail without my help."

You look at the reptilian humanoid. Is it smiling at you through the glass? You look at Quinn on the floor, dead, her jumpsuit completely red.

You can just bolt, head out of there. The keys to the van are in the ignition, you remember that part of the plan. And you saw the keys there before you got out. Right?

"You won't survive alone," you hear the voice say. "You need me."

You have both GoPro cameras, your colleagues are dead, that's it, you're out of there. Leaping over the bodies of Jonas and Amos and both security guards down the hallway, you find yourself at the laboratory door and step outside.

But then you pause. You can't leave them, those prisoners, can you? The humans at least? Or should you also free the reptilian humanoid? What if it's right, and you won't survive alone? And if you did, could you handle the guilt of leaving those innocents behind?

Make a run for it, turn to page 110.
Free the prisoners, turn to page 141.

You awake startled but groggy. You're lying in a bed in what looks like a very small hotel room. You sit up but the quick movement makes you dizzy. There's a bottle of water on the table by the bed and you quickly grab it, open it, and drink down the whole thing. Your hands and limbs feel heavy and your chest is bruised but otherwise you feel ok.

You stand, then rock back and forth for a moment, another dizzy spell. Or is it? The whole room seems to be swaying. And why is there no window in this room? You move towards the door and try the handle. It's locked.

Suddenly, the door opens.

Standing in the doorway is one of the biggest men you've ever seen. He's bigger than the doorway really. And he's wearing a tuxedo?

"How are you feeling?" he asks in a deep voice.

"Ok I guess," you say. "Where am I?"

"Follow me," the man says and walks away.

You step out of the room into a long, skinny hallway to follow the tuxedoed brute. His shoulders are as wide as the hallway and with his height his head just barely misses the ceiling. Lumbering along, he leads you further and further down this wood-paneled hallway, past a few doors that look like your door to a door at the end of the hallway. He opens it and steps outside while motioning for you to follow him.

It's dark outside. Have you been asleep for a full day?

You step out and there's nothing but sky and stars and it's very windy. You're standing on the deck of a massive luxury yacht that out at sea. You can smell the salt air. The cool wind is invigorating and for a moment you feel calm, at peace.

"This way," the man says, trudging along.

Farther away, towards where you're being led, you can see a group of people seated around a collection of large tables. They're eating dinner maybe? It looks something like a wedding reception. As you approach, yes, you can see they are having a formal dinner with LED candles and a small swarm of servers dressed all in black clearing plates and pouring wine. Someone laughs and someone says something else and then they all laugh. One of them looks familiar? Another one looks up and sees you, then stands and hurriedly walks over to you.

"You're up!" he says. He's also wearing a tuxedo. They all are. "I'm so glad. No hard feelings about that tranquilizer I hope." It's the man with the cap from the boat at Poets Beach. "We just couldn't risk having you awake on the initial journey and all, you understand."

"You shot me," you say.

"It was a bloody dart," he says. "Don't get snobby. Come, let me introduce you to everyone." He leads you towards the table and excuses the large man with a simple, "Thank you."

"You're welcome, Doctor Wexler," he says.

"Wexler?" you ask.

"Oh yes," he says. "A proper introduction, of course. My name is Nicholas Wexler. And I am the project manager, so to speak, of this adventure. Come, let me introduce you, everyone is very excited to meet you."

Doctor Wexler walks you towards the large group, all of whom are dressed formally, men in tuxedos and women in sparkly gowns, and, wait – one of them looks just like Mark Zuckerberg.

"Ladies and gentlemen," Wexler says loudly. "If I may have your attention? It is my great honor to introduce you to our newest crew member, our great, good samaritan, our--"

"He looks like a member of Antifa!" one of the men says, getting laughs from everyone.

You now realize you're wearing all black, black hoodie and black jeans, next to Welxer in his tuxedo and everyone else's formal wear.

"Oh, E," says one of the women. "Just for once, don't be an asshole." Everyone laughs some more.

"Let me be the first to say, 'Welcome aboard,'" says one of the men, holding up a glass of wine. It's Jeff Bezos.

A chorus of additional welcomes and cheers follow as you begin to recognize more of the guests at the table... the brash "E" with the Antifa joke is none other than Elon Musk, and the woman who chided him? She stands, takes two glasses of wine and walks towards you.

"This is Grimes," says, Wexler.

"Claire," she says, handing you one of the glasses of wine. "Please, call me Claire," and clinks your glass with her glass.

"Right," Wexler says. "Claire, yes, of course."

Now pointing with his open palm, Wexler goes around the table with his introductions: "Jeff and Lauren, certainly. Bill and Melinda with Rory, Phoebe, and Jennifer." They nod and smile and Welxer continues. "This Bernard, Antoine, Delphine, Frederic, Jean… Warren and Susan, Peter, Graham. Here is Larry and Nikita, Megan, David… Amancio, Flora, Marta, Sandra, Marcos… Mark and Priscilla… and, of course, Jim, Alice, and Rob Walton." He concludes the introductions with a gentle applause, which seems weird because he's the only one clapping.

"We're the richest people in the world," says Mark Zuckerberg. "Don't you recognize us!"

And once again everyone at the table erupts in laughter. Are they drunk? You take a sip from your wine.

"Don't worry," Grimes tells you. "We're not all terrible." She winks and returns to her seat.

"Please," says Melinda Gates. "Sit. Join us."

Suddenly a flurry of servers produce a chair and place setting out of seemingly nowhere and you sit at the table between Grimes and one of Amancio Ortega's children, you presume. Doctor Wexler returns to his seat across the table.

"You must be hungry," Jeff Bezos says. "What would you like to eat?"

This is all happening so quickly. "Um," you say. "What's on the menu?"

Everyone bursts into laughter.

"Whatever the fuck you want!" yelps the teenage girl seated next to Melinda.

Everyone laughs again.

"Phoebe," Bill Gates says. "There's no need to curse."

"Phoebe," Elon Musk says. "There's no need to fuckin' curse."

Grimes leans in while the others laugh and whispers to you, "You can have anything you'd like, just tell them what you want." She leans back and you notice a server standing patiently by your side.

"Bring him the swordfish," says Larry Ellisson. "And I'll have a slice of chocolate cake."

"I'll also have the cake," says Sam Walton.

"I like cake," says Bill Gates.

"Who doesn't like cake?" asks Amancio Ortega.

"Oh, no," says Lauren Sanchez. "It's just too rich for me."

Elon Musk slaps his hand on the table and howls with laughter, saying, "Too rich she says!" And the rest of them join in the laughter.

Grimes leans in towards you again, saying, "If you don't like fish, you can have steak." But then she grimaces. "Oh, sorry, unless you're vegan? Vegetarian?"

You shake your head no.

"How about I order for you?" she asks.

You nod.

"I also like rich cake!" announces Mark Zuckerberg.

"Cake is great!" says Warren Buffett.

Grimes motions for the server to come to her and whispers an order then gives you another wink.

"Where are we?" you ask Grimes.

She just smiles and shrugs, taking a big sip from her wine.

"I'm curious," announces Amancio Ortega, now having the attention of everyone at the table. "What made you decide to join us on this voyage?"

You realize he's talking to you.

"Well," Doctor Wexler says. "You see, we, uh, maybe we should save these kinds of discussions for after dinner? I'm sure we all have questions, but let's allow our guest to dine first shall we?"

"Si, mi angelito," says Flora Perez Marcode. "Déjalo comer, déjalo comer..."

Amancio nods while frowning.

"Qu'ils mangent de la brioche!" yells Grimes.

And everyone laughs. Elon Musk, leans over and gives Grimes a kiss on the forehead and whispers something in her ear.

Now, a number of servers are placing small porcelain plates with large wedges of chocolate cake on the table in front of everyone, including you. Everyone begins to eat almost immediately, moaning with joy and pleasure from the taste of the cake. You're hungry now but cake does not feel very appetizing.

"In South India," says Bill Gates with a mouthful of cake, chewing, then swallowing. "In South India they eat their dessert first."

You pick up your fork to take a bite of cake. Suddenly, a hand from behind you moves the cake plate towards the center of the table while another hand from the other side places a new plate before you, featuring a thinly sliced steak, a bright red lobster, green beans, and a large baked potato filled with sour cream, bacon bits, chives, and shredded cheddar cheese.

"Surf and turf!" announces Grimes, proud of herself, smiling at you with black cake in her teeth.

"And a baked potato with all the fixings," says Priscilla Chan now holding hands on the table with Mark Zuckerberg.

"All the fixings," Zuckerberg says, raising his glass.

Everyone raises their glasses saying, "All the fixings!"

You raise your glass as well, and Grimes leans over and rather forcibly clinks your glass.

Everyone continueus to eat their cake.

You begin to eat your steak and lobster and baked potato and everything is delicious. You're hungrier than you thought. You take another sip from your wine and as soon as you put the glass down on the table a server refills it. Your eyes meet those of Doctor Wexler who smiles at you as if to say congratulations. You smile and nod as if to say thank you.

This is great. But still, very weird. And you can't help but feel a little bit like you've been kidnapped. Part of you wants to scream at them and demand some answers. Another part of you wants to just relax and enjoy the ride. All in good time, right? Right?

Play it cool and try to relax, turn to page 113.
Put your foot down and demand answers, turn to page 122.

"I didn't hear anything," you say.

"The creature didn't communicate with you?" asks the tall, skinny man.

"No, it didn't," you say.

"Nothing at all?"

"Nothing," you say.

The tall, skinny man raises the pistol to your face and fires. The back of your head explodes, splattering on the wall behind you.

You did not survive 2020.

THE END

The plan is to kidnap high ranking members of the military. If they think they can attack us like they did in Lafayette Square and not expect retaliation, they're wrong.

It's a big move, ambitious and certainly illegal. You play along, supporting the leadership, but sticking to the periphery of the planning and activities.

Ultimately, you join as part of the HQ team. You and Beau are tasked to stay at the house to receive and retain the kidnapped. There will be two attack teams out in the streets, tailing targets, taking action, and bringing the targets back to the house.

"Here," one of the new protestors says to you as everyone is heading out. "Take this." And he hands you a Glock handgun.

You quietly accept the gun and tuck it into the waistline of your pants.

You and Beau are alone in the house for just a couple of hours before the door bursts open and Team A comes barreling inside with a bound and gagged middle aged white man.

"Keep him in the basement," you're told.

So you and Beau drag this man down into the basement and sit him in a chair. At first you're feeling pretty good, righteous even. But then you feel a bit of pity for this man so you ungag him. And then he starts talking, saying that you'll never get away with this, and they'll come for him, and they'll put you in Guantanamo Bay for what you're doing to him.

Then Beau punches him hard in the face. "Fuck you, you fuckin' fascist!" he says.

The man spits blood but then starts laughing. "That's the problem with you people," he says. "You think this is about you and your freedoms, your BLM protests, your votes, your rights. You're blind to what is really going on. We are heading into a new era, a new world order! The powers that be have spoken. Our President will lead us into a final war against the deviants, the Satanists, the pedeophiles… These people are the real problem in this world and we're the ones to stop them!"

"By attacking peaceful protestors?" Beau yells.

"By any means necessary!" this man yells back. "You don't know what's at stake here. Your shitty little lives mean nothing compared to what's really going on. You call Q a hoax, you say the Deep State is a conspiracy, aliens don't exist, climate change is real… you think you know everything! You don't know shit. Soon enough you'll get sick, your parents will get sick, everyone you know will get sick and then they'll die. We're thinning the herd, starting with the weakest ones. We're doing you a favor, really! Otherwise, what? You work some shitty job for the rest of your life worrying about rent and car insurance or buying diapers for some ugly kid because you knocked up some bimbo. Look at you! You're pathetic. Your life is pitiful. You have *nothing*, you are *nothing*, your parents were *nothing*, and your children will be *NOTHING!*"

You pull out your gun and press the muzzle against this man's forehead.

"Yo!" says Beau.

The middle aged white man laughs at you. "You think you're tough? You think you got what it takes to kill someone? Go ahead. Do it. Do it!"

"Gimme the gun," Beau says.

"At least I have the guts to fight for what I believe in, to give everything," the man says. "You're not even worth the taxes we get from you."

"Give me the goddamn gun," Beau says...

Shoot him, turn to page 116.
Give Beau the gun, turn to page 134.

Outside on this loading dock with your white van right there, you take a moment to survey the scene. Everything is still and quiet. But anyone nearby would've heard the gunshots. Is there no one else here?

You can't waste any more time. You need to get out of here, but to where? Do you take the van and head make a run for it? Stick with the plan and bike to Sutherland's place?

Try the van, turn to page 117.

Stick to the plan and head to the bicycle, turn to page 144.

"Ok," you say. "Show me."

"This way," he says, leading you in the opposite direction than you planned to go. "I'm Jim. The rest of us are over here."

Together you move through the foliage, careful to avoid the paths as best you can. You come upon a small clearing where you find five more men dressed as police officers. They're armed with pistols and automatic rifles.

"Who's this?" one of them says.

"Don't worry," Jim says. "What did you find?"

"It's almost time," one of them says. "The aliens have descended and they're meeting with the generals."

"Just like we predicted," Jim mumbles. "Ok, this is it. Stick with the plan."

The group leaves the clearing, moving quickly towards an area from where you can see bright lights in an open field, Sheep Meadow. You follow, falling behind, but running to keep up.

You catch up with them at the treeline of the open field. At one end of the field you can see where the light is coming from: a military command post with tents and generators and armored vehicles and dozens of soldiers.

On the other side, towards the center of the field, you can see the aliens: three tall, slender, grey aliens with large heads and black, almond-shaped eyes, towering over a small group of military generals. It looks like they're talking but from where you are you can't hear anything.

You look at your group of imposter police, all poised for action. One of them raises a sniper rifle and aims it at the meeting of generals and aliens. Just as you realize what's happening, one of the alien's heads explodes from the gunshot. Its towering body waivers for a moment and crumples to the ground leaving the other aliens standing, stunned, their heads splattered with the green blood of their fallen companion.

The imposter cops run to the field from the treeline screaming and shooting at the aliens and generals. Two of the generals are shot and fall.

Suddenly, a piercing scream, something like a shrieking siren, blocks out all other sounds and a number of green laser beams extend from the bottom of the craft simultaneously targeting the police imposters and the command center, sweeping across the field, crisscrossing, and cutting through everything they touch: armored vehicles, soldiers, the attacking police imposters are sliced in half in mid step their body parts scattering among the singed grass.

The lazers mow down everything, everyone, including you hiding in the tree line.

You did not survive 2020.

THE END

It seems like at least the doctor is on your side. And hell, as long as you're in the company of these billionaires, you can't be in that much danger. You down your glass of wine and watch as a server immediately refills it.

The evening continues with more wine and more food and more cake and while many of the guests "retire for the evening" or "head to our cabin", a few of you remain on deck drinking and eating and everything is, well, everything is wonderful. And everyone, including you, is drunk.

"I didn't even really want a baby," Grimes tells you. "But also, like, I really really really wanted a baby, ya know?"

You smile and nod.

"What do you think of the others? You'll probably have to make a baby with one of them when we get there."

"Where are we going?" you ask.

"Too many questions!"

"I just want to know where we're going!" you say.

Suddenly, Elon Musk butts into your conversation, saying, "You'll find you when we get there!!"

"Get where?" you ask.

Doctor Wexler joins your conversation, saying, "I think that's about enough for one night, don't you?"

"Where the hell are we going?" you ask.

"Oh just shut the hell up," Musk says.

"Screw you!" you say.

"Ok, that's enough," Musk says, motioning to someone behind you.

"You'll be fine," Doctor Wexler tells you.

"Huh?" you ask, and suddenly you're lifted out of your chair by two enormous men who very easily carry you away from the table. You scream and fight but it makes no use.

The men place you on a gurney and strap you down: your legs, your arms, your head. You can't move at all. All you can do is scream.

Doctor Wexler comes running up to you. "Just something to calm you down," he says. "I'm sorry." And you feel a prick in your neck and very quickly everything fades to black.

You wake up in your same cabin room again, lying there

in bed. Did that dinner really happen?

You stand, walk to the door, and gently try the doorknob. It's locked.

You sit back down to see if the giant tuxedoed man returns. If that indeed happened. But nothing happens, no one comes.

There's no clock, no windows, nothing to indicate what time it is, what day it is, or even where you may be. But one thing is different: there's no movement, no swaying. Perhaps the boat has docked?

How much time has passed? How long have you even been in here?

You try the door again. Locked. You bang on the door and shout to be let out. Nothing.

Try to pick the lock, turn to page 131.
Stay calm, remain patient, turn to page 139.

Ascension. With just a positive thought of confirmation, you're suddenly falling backwards in your chair into a mass of thick blackness that soon gives way to an intense heat and blinding white light.

In what feels like both a lifetime and a mere second, you're exposed to all the workings of the world, the evolution of the planet, humanity's rise to great influence, war, poverty, disease, natural disasters. You're not merely watching this, but experiencing it as well. The pain and sorrow of humanity's evils and atrocities pass through you and then space and time disappear.

You are nothing. You are nowhere.

There is only emptiness.

Then there is space, vast and infinite. A star collapses in on itself to create a black hole. Another star and a billion more do the same. Matter and space dust and gasses and ice pass and collect and combine and break and then a stillness, a calm. The serenity of space envelopes you.

Now you're one among the extraterrestrials. Their minds are your mind and their past is your past is your present is their present and your future together. You are in the fourth dimension. You understand the laws of the cosmos. You can see time. You can shape space. You are where you want to be, when you want to be.

You now understand all the secrets of the universe. You are like the extraterrestrials, living outside of time and space. You have ascended. You are a different entity now.

You have become, what humans would call, a god.

Congratulations, you have survived 2020.

THE END

You squeeze the trigger and the man's head explodes, splattering blood everywhere, all over your face and chest.

The sound of the gunshot reverberates in the basement and your ears are ringing.

For a moment that's all there is: only the ringing.

"Jesus," Beau says.

But this is just the first blood to be spilled. Soon, the protests and riots will turn to full-on battles with violence and bloodshed on both sides. This man you killed will be heralded as a martyr and you will be celebrated as a revolutionary by your respective sides.

Now, it is war.

And you become the leader of the revolution.

As the war rages on, you continue to fight with the people, to push back the rising tides of Fascism, Authoritarianism, and the idiocracy of racists and red sheeple.

This second American Civil War is dark and deadly. And, hell... from where you are now, there is no end in sight.

But one thing is for certain: you survived 2020, and lived to continue this fight for justice.

THE END

Take the fastest way possible!

You jump off the loading dock, open the van door, climb in, and close the door behind you. The keys are in the ignition, yes! You start up the van, shift into reverse, circle around to face the direction you drove in, and shift into drive.

Again, you pause.

Are you really going to leave those people imprisoned?

Drive away, turn to page 130.
Free the prisoners, turn to page 141.

ACAB, real or fake. You take off running into the park. You follow a path for a while and then tuck into a bushy area to catch your breath and see if he's following you. There's nothing. You keep going, now slowly, listening, as you head deeper into the park. Still, you hear nothing but there is a light, a brighter light coming through the park and not from the craft.

Making your way towards the light, you can see that it's coming from an open field, Sheep Meadow. Careful not to step out into the open, you stay off the paths and make your way closer and closer to the field light.

There, in the middle of the meadow is a military command station, with bright lights and generators, tents, armored vehicles, soldiers. Everyone seems to be listless, bored?

But wait, now something is happening with the craft. The underbelly is shimmering, rippling between matte grey and reflective silver. The underbelly is opening, revealing a bright aqua glow from inside. The light then intensifies and descends to the field like falling water in a tubular shape. Maybe fifty yards from the military command center this tube of light touches down on the field. It grows brighter, too bright, and you have to look away, then the light is gone

As your eyes adjust, you can make out three figures standing in the middle of the field. It's the extraterrestrials.

The aliens are grey, extremely tall, slender, with long limbs and large heads with black, almond-shaped eyes.

Three military men walk out into the field and head towards the aliens. They're unarmed and seemingly unafraid, and stop to stand just 10 feet from the aliens who are nearly twice as tall as the men. The men speaking to the aliens but you can't hear what they're saying.

"Yes," you hear a strange voice say. It's quiet, omnidirectional, almost like it's coming from inside you. "We have returned." The aliens are speaking telepathically, seemingly to everyone there?

"The experiment is now concluded," the voice says. "Our agreement ends now. Your greed, masked as progress, has gone unchecked for long enough. We have allowed your wars, your torture, your stockpiling while others starve. The crimes of man against man are... expected. But your crimes against this planet have compelled us to intervene. Now is a time of great change. Humanity, if it is to survive, must be made to reconcile. Right now, many more of us are communicating this to the many factions of your leadership. Today is the last day of nationalism and strife on this planet. Your weapons are now rendered useless. Your money is now worthless. Everything that you've known to be true and real will now be revealed as construct and conjecture. Together, we will thrive. No one will be hungry, no one will be sick. This initial transition will be difficult for many, but in time, this planet will be remedied, your actions rectified. And all will thrive. All of you. Now, lay down your arms and approach us. Come, lay down your arms."

The military men meeting with the aliens look back to the command center troops who are now, trepidatiously placing their guns on the ground and approaching the aliens.

"And the rest of you," says the voice, as the three aliens extend their long, slender arms towards the outskirts of the meadow. "You too shall reveal yourselves. Come together."

You watch as a few people step out of the treeline surrounding the field and walk towards the aliens.

"Come," the voice says. "Come together."

More and more people, people like you who somehow made their way here and were silently watching from the bushes, reveal themselves and make their way across the field.

"Your old world is done and gone," the voice says. "You have lost your privileges. You will now follow our leadership."

One of the aliens faces the military men and slowly moves his hand across the field, an action that somehow surgically decapitates the three military men. Their bodies crumple to the ground.

"Those who oppose us will die," the voice says. "Those who reject us will suffer. Those who follow us will be rewarded. WE. ARE. YOUR. NEW. GODS."

Congratulations, you've survived 2020. At least this far...

THE END

"It said to kill the guards," you say.

"What else?" the tall, skinny man asks.

"That's it," you say.

"What else?" the tall, skinny man asks again.

"That's all it said, that's all," you say.

"Nothing about the virus?"

"The virus?

"Nothing about COVID?"

"No," you say.

"Well," the tall, skinny man says. "We may still have use for you yet." He raises his gun into the air and brings it down fast, hitting you in the head, right in the temple with the butt of the handle knocking you unconscious.

When you awake, you're sitting in another laboratory room, similar but different than where you were. Or is it? You're in a large metal chair, something like a barbershop chair and you quickly realize that your hands and legs are bound to the chair.

Across the room from you is the reptilian humanoid also bound to a large, metal chair.

The tall, skinny man stands beside you.

"What happens now is very simple," the man says. "You're going to tell me what the creature tells you. I will ask the questions, the creature will answer, and you will repeat those answers."

"Where am I?" you ask, wriggling in your restraints. "What is this–"

Suddenly, your entire body spasms and tenses and the pain is excruciating. It feels like your insides are on fire and you're paralyzed. Then, it stops, and you're left panting in your chair.

"You didn't let me finish," the tall, skinny man says. "I find that electricuition is the best means of coercion so that's what we'll be using here today. But don't worry. If the creature tells you what we want to know, then I won't electrocute you."

"This is crazy," you say. "Please!"

The electricity once again ignites your entire body and your jaw clamps down biting the tip of your tongue clean off. Then it's over.

"You're wasting time!" the man says. "Ask the creature to tell you the truth."

"What is the truth?" you say with a mouthful of blood.

The creature stares back at you in silence.

"Please!" you ask. "What is the truth?"

The creature cocks its head to one side and then you hear, "Do you really think this man will let you live? Even if I told you what he wants to hear?"

"Please!" you yell. "Whatever he wants, please, tell us!"

The creature's head straightens, but then nothing.

"You're not doing a very good job, are you?" asks the tall, skinny man right before he electrocutes you again, this time for longer, what feels like forever, like it may never end, and then miraculously it does.

"Stop…" you say. "Stop…"

But he electrocutes you again.

"Please!" you scream, crying, sobbing, blood spilling from your mouth.

"Last chance," the man says.

You stare at the creature who sits motionless, emotionless. You beg in silence. A moment passes and finally you hear the voice say, "I'm sorry."

"Nooooo!" you scream.

The electricity passes through you seizing your body and in the moment all you know is pain and agony and then it's over. It's all over.

You did not survive 2020.

"Bring me the other human communicator," the tall, skinny man says. "Maybe we'll do better with him."

THE END

“I’m sorry,” you say. “This is all really great, and I’m just wondering...”

Everyone stops eating and looks at you.

“You’re wondering what the hell you’re doing here,” says Elon Musk.

“Yeah,” you say. “What the hell am I doing here?”

Everyone laughs.

“You’re our slave boy,” Grimes says.

“Don’t say that,” says Bill Gates.

“Tu es chanceux,” says Bernard Arnault.

“You are one in one hundred million,” says Mark Zuckerberg.

“You’re the cure for COVID,” yelps Elon Musk.

“Well,” says Doctor Wexler. “Not exactly the cure but... yes, potentially. If I may?”

The guests at the table do not object.

“The truth is,” Doctor Wexler says, “despite what the government says, it will be extremely difficult to make a vaccine for the Coronavirus.”

“Impossible,” says Elon Musk.

“Nearly impossible,” says Bill Gates.

A moment of silence fills the air.

“Millions and millions more will die,” says Doctor Wexler. “But there are some people, very, very few, who have an unexplained immunity to the virus. And we believe these people are our best chance at beating this. These people are really the only hope for the future that we have. These people, people like you...”

“You are immune to the Coronavirus,” says Warren Buffett. “That’s why you’re here.”

“That’s why you’re coming with us,” says Elon Musk.

“We need you,” says Doctor Wexler.

“And you need us,” says Bill Gates. “We can help you.”

“Right now,” says Doctor Wexler, “We’re on our way to a secure location, a laboratory and medical center, where we can do the important work that needs to be done. This is all very clandestine, of course. I’m sure you can imagine how important this work is, and how important you are.”

"We're scheduled to arrive around noon tomorrow," Musk says. "And then it's time to get to work!"

"Arrive where exactly?"

"That's top secret," Grimes says, smiling.

"We have a facility," Jeff Bezos says. "It's a floating facility over the Tufts plain, about 1,200 miles west of Seattle."

"It's extraordinary," says Warren Buffett.

"We'll have everything we need there," says Doctor Wexler. "Everyone has their own accommodations and top of the line amenities."

"For how long?" you ask.

Everyone laughs.

"He's funny," says Bill Gates.

"We have our contingency plans," Prescilla Chan says. "Right, sweetie?"

"That's right, dumpling," says Mark Zuckerberg. "We've been closely monitoring the spread of COVID as well as increasing political instability, rising inequality, and the imminent climate catastrophe, and our data says--"

"We're fucked," Grimes says.

"Not true!" says Elon Musk.

"Yes," Jeff Bezos says. "*They're* fucked."

And everyone laughs.

"That's funny," says Bill Gates.

"If it gets really, really bad," says Grimes. "We'll just go to the moon!"

"To the moon!" says Warren Buffett.

"To the moon!" the rest say in unison, raising their glasses.

"You didn't eat your cake," says Bill Gates.

"What?" you ask, stunned by what you're learning.

"It's ok, honey," says Melinda Gates. "Not everyone eats their cake."

"We're all done here," announces Larry Ellison and motions to the group of servers standing watch. "Clear the table, will ya?"

A swarm of black-clad servers descend upon the table grabbing plates and utensils. You can't help but think they look like ninjas. Are they all Asian? One grabs your plate with an untouched slice of cake.

"Don't take that without asking first!" yelps Elon Musk.

"I'm sorry," says the young, Chinese waitress. She looks directly into your eyes and asks, "Are you finished?" She winks.

"Yes?" you say, and the server clears your cake plate.

"I'll be honest," Jim Walton says to you. "This is the best thing that's ever happened to you. You'll never have to worry about anything for the rest of your life."

"Or until we don't need you anymore," Grimes says.

"Stop that!" says Melinda Gates.

"She's not wrong," says Bill Gates.

"So let me get this straight," you say. "With my COVID immunity, you think you'll be able to make a vaccine on your own?"

"Maybe," says Jeff Bezos. "There's also opportunities for plasma therapy, dialysis, stem cell research, CRISPR therapeutics..."

"We've done our research," says Mark Zuckerberg.

"You'll be very well taken care of," says Doctor Wexler.

"What about my parents?" you ask. "My family?"

No one speaks.

"And if I say no?" you ask.

"You don't want to say no," Grimes says, and burps.

"Wow," says Bill Gates.

"May I have some water?" orders Jeff Bezos. He looks very sweaty.

"Yes," says Lauren Sanchez. "Water, please." She too looks sweaty, and pale.

Suddenly, one of the Gates' children, Phoebe, stands up and violently vomits on the table. Another one, Rory, nearly falls out of his chair trying to excuse himself only to stumble a few feet before vomiting on the deck.

"What the fuck!" screams Grimes.

Everyone is aghast, moaning and groaning, standing up and backing away.

"Children," Bill Gates says. "Are you ok?"

The third Gates child, Jennifer, stands and announces, "I'm going to be sick too!" Then turns to face away from the table but she's not fast enough and projectile vomits all over her mother, Melinda Gates, before collapsing to the ground. Melinda, now covered in black vomit, then gags and gags again before cupping her hands to try and catch her own vomit.

BIll Gates groans and vomits and collapses.

Jeff Bezos and Lauren Sanchez desperately cling to each other as they burp and belch, sobbing, with a slow trickle of black sludge dribbling from the corners of their mouths.

The Waltons, Jim, Alice, and Rob, now standing in shock of the scene, seem fine but then Alice screams, "Oh, no!" And hikes up her gown to squat and releases a deluge of diarrhea right there on the deck. As she cries, Jim and Rob, as white as their white tuxedo shirts, both projectile vomit black sludge before folding over and collapsing. Alice, still squatting, vomits and keels over.

Warren Buffett is making strange gurgling sounds.

"Daddy!" says Buffett's daughter Susan coming to his aid as black ooze slowly bubbles out of his mouth and down his chest. Almost immediately Susan gags and vomits then falls to her knees. Peter Buffett and Graham Buffet stand in shock but then both double over clutching their stomachs and shit their pants as black goo drips from their mouths.

"C'est la vie," says Bernard Arnault just before he too projectile vomits like water from a firehouse directly into the faces of all four of his children who then fall out of their chairs and writhe and trash around on the deck expunging slushy, black slime from all of their oravices.

Larry Ellison belches, which prompts Nikita Kahn to clasp her hands on his mouth as if to keep the vomit inside him. But she vomits all over him. And then he vomits all over her. Larry's children Megan and David scream only to start choking and aspirating on their own vomit before dropping dead with two thuds.

Rosalia Mera, belching with tears in her eyes, slaps Amancio Ortega repeatedly, screaming, "Pelotudo de mierda! Pelotudo de mierda!" Amancio Ortega's three children then attack Rosalia Mera, pummeling her with fists and pulling at her hair until all four of them fall to the ground in a flurry of fisticuffs, a swirling mass of black slop and limbs that suddenly goes limp and still.

Amancio Ortega simply expires with a long, cacophonous flatulence as his eyes roll backwards.

Now, the dozen servers, all dressed in black, stand in a semicircle watching this whole scene unfold. A few brutish muscle men in tuxedos come running but a pair of servers quickly subdue them with some fierce karate moves. In seconds the muscle men are unconscious on the deck and one of the servers zipties their hands and feet together.

Lauren Sanchez, bug-eyed and dribbling black ooze from her mouth, breaks free of her embrace with Jeff Bezos and runs straight for the port side of the yacht and throws herself overboard.

Bezos stands up, mildly convulsing as black sludge leaking from his mouth. He buttons his suit jacket.

You and Musk and Grimes sit there watching in awe.

The ship now seems to have picked up speed, kicking up sea spray as the wind whips across the open deck.

One of the servers, a woman with short black hair, steps forward from the group. She's clearly their leader. She locks eyes with Jeff Bezos.

"Hello, Ba Jiao Gui," Bezos says, sputtering.

"Hello, Bezos," says Ba Jiao Gui in a strange, supernatural voice that seems to come not from her but from all around you, like some kind of celestial surround sound. "I have come to collect."

"I'm surprised it's taken you this long," says Bezos.

"Time is a human construct," says Ba Jiao Gui. "But yes, you had your chance, and plenty of *time*."

Jeff Bezos spits out a glob of black goo. "You shouldn't have done it this way," he says. "All these people?"

"You care not for people," says Ba Jiao Gui. "Your *greed* has killed these people. Your broken promise has killed these people."

Some of the servers break from the semicircle and move towards you at the table. Each one of them aims a pistol at your remaining group: Grimes, Musk, the Zuckerbergs, and you. The Zuckerbergs look frightened, but Musk and Grimes seem unaffected, calm.

"Approach me," Ba Jiao Gui orders Bezos.

He remains still.

"*Approach me!*" says Ba Jiao Gui and the words echo in the air like thunder.

Bezos walks, slowly, one step at a time, towards her and then suddenly Ba Jiao Gui moves so quickly it's almost a blur as she lunges at Bezos and then returns to her initial position a few feet away. They both stand in silence staring at each other. And then you see it: Bezos's stomach has been sliced open and his intestines hang down spooling into a knotted coil at his feet.

Now wide-eyed and in shock, Bezos looks down at his stomach and begins to gently attempt to push his intestines back into his gutted abdomen. Ba Jiao Gui walks, almost glides, across the deck to Bezos where she squats down before him.

She gathers a length of his bloody intestines and steps to move behind him. Then, with a swift kick to the back of his legs, she drops him to his knees.

A lightning bolt splinters across the sky immediately followed by a deafening thunder clap and suddenly it begins to rain, torrential rain, sheets of rain, and more lightning.

Ba Jiao Gui wraps Bezos's lengthy intestines around her hands and then gently coils the middle slack around his neck, once, twice, three times. Tightening the slack, she yanks back hard strangling Bezos with the length of his intestines as he desperately flails his arms trying to reach back at her. Another strobic flash of lightning shows the sheets of rain pummeling his purple face, his eyes bulging from their sockets, his mouth open and screaming but not making a sound.

And then it's done: Bezos's arms collapse by his sides and his body goes limp. A deafening thunderclap ripples through the air. Ba Jiao Gui releases her grip on the choke rope of his intestines, letting Bezos fall face first onto the deck with the thud of dead weight.

Ba Jiao Gui, with bloody hands, looks up to the sky and opens her mouth, tongue out, to catch the rain. She stands in stillness.

Lightning streaks across the sky and a thunderclap rattles your very bones.

"Whoa," says Grimes, her hair now wet and matted to her head.

Mark Zuckerberg and Priscilla Chan sit there soaking wet, but otherwise unfazed. "Very impressive," Mark says.

"You ate the cake, though!" yells Elon Musk. "They ate the cake!"

"It will take more than poison to kill us," says Priscilla Chan as lightning splinters across the sky.

"Still," Mark Zuckerberg says. "Very impressive."

Suddenly, Mark Zuckerberg's forehead explodes from a gunshot. Only the lower half of his face remains. Priscilla screams and then her face explodes from another gunshot. Both bodies stay seated upright for a moment, but then keel over onto the table where their heads lie open and exposed to the world.

Elon Musk stands holding a smoking Glock pistol aimed at the Zuckerbergs.

"What the fuck, Elon!" screams Grimes.

"How the hell are they immune to poison?" Elon asks no one in particular.

"What the fuck?" screams Grimes. "What the fuck?"

"Don't worry, baby," Elon says. "It's all part of the plan."

"What plan?" Grimes screams.

Now, the sound of a baby crying can be heard. One of the Chinese servers is walking out onto the deck with a small baby.

"What are you doing with my baby?" Grimes screams, standing to run towards the child, but Elon grabs her, wrapping his arms around her holding her while she kicks and screams.

The server hands the baby to Ba Jiao Gui.

"Don't you touch him!" screams Grimes, furiously writhing in Musk's arms.

Ba Jiao Gui, looks down at the child, gently rocking him as he cries while the rain pelts his face.

"We had a deal, Ba Jiao!" says Musk.

"Yes," Ba Jiao Gui says. "We had a deal." Then, she holds out the crying baby in her outstretched arms.

Musk releases Grimes who runs to Ba Jiao Gui and retrieves her baby boy holding him close to her chest walking backwards to Musk with tears in her eyes.

"You have twenty minutes," says Ba Jiao Gui.

"Thank you," Musk says. Then he looks at you. "Let's go," he says.

"What?" you ask.

"Let's go!" Musk says. "The ship is going down and we're taking the escape pod."

"What?" asks Grimes.

"It's all part of the plan," Musk says. "The ship sinks, and we're the survivors. We'll get picked up and brought to the lab in the morning."

"The *plan*?" Grimes asks.

"I'll explain everything in the pod," Musk says. "We need to move."

"What are you talking about?" Grimes says. "What the fuck is happening?"

"Let's go!" Musk says. "We're leaving!"

Lightning flashes across the sky illuminating Ba Jiao Gui and her horde.

"You can come with us," Ba Jiao Gui says to you. "You are welcome where we are going."

"What?" Musk screams. "No way!" He looks at you and points his gun at you. "You're coming with us."

"You are welcome with us," Ba Jiao Gui says.

"Shut up!" Musk tells her. Then to you, he says, "You're coming with us!"

A thunderclap reverberates through the sky.

"Let's go!" says Musk.

"Make your choice," says Ba Jiao Gui.

Go with Elon Musk in the escape pod, turn to page 136.
Stay with Ba Jiao Gui, turn to page 147.

You're not going to make it if you don't leave now.

You floor the gas pedal and the van lurches forward. You drive through the small service roads of the Navy Yard towards the entrance. Then, you can see the gate, you're almost there!

Suddenly, a half dozen large, black SUVs speed up Flushing Avenue to the gated entrance and screech to a halt. You're driving at top speed with the gas pedal pressed to the floor as you watch a number of men in black suits jump out of the SUVs and take aim at you with automatic firearms.

Do you hit the brakes and try for another exit? Or keep your momentum and try to drive through the blockade?

Try to crash through the blockade, turn to page 135.
Hit the brakes and try another way out, turn to page 142.

Enough is enough. There's no way you're just going to sit in here and wait for who knows what to happen to you. Looking around the room, there isn't too much to find that could be useful to pick the lock. There's nothing more than a bed with sheets, the sink and toilet… looking at the door, it doesn't seem too sturdy actually. You wonder if you could just break it open somehow.

You position yourself in front of the door and with all your strength you raise your leg and kick the door with your heel. Nothing. You try again, kicking close to the doorknob. Nothing. You try again. And again. And again. And again. Nothing.

Now panting, bent over, you're not ready to give up, but maybe need to reevaluate your strategy.

Then, the door gently opens. Standing there in the hallway is a woman dressed in all black. One of the servers perhaps? She looks at you for a moment and then simply walks away leaving the door open.

You peer out into the hallway to see her turn down another corridor and out of sight. You quietly step out of the room and move down the hallway following her.

"Hey," you hear someone say.

You turn and see one of the large muscle men who subdued you earlier. "Where do you think you're going," he says.

You take off running down the hallway and you can hear him running after you. You turn down one corridor, then another, and he's still chasing you.

At the end of this hallway you see a swinging kitchen door and you push through into a large, fluorescent-lit, professional kitchen with shiny stainless steel counters and appliances. In the center of the kitchen are four black-clad servers, wearing balaclavas, loading uzis with long clips of bullets and twisting large silencing tubes onto the gun muzzles.

They freeze and look at you.

You instinctively hunch over and raise your hands as the muscle man slams through the swinging door behind you. He sees you and the group of armed servers in ski masks.

"What the–" he mutters before being violently peppered with bullets and collapsing to the floor in a bloody lump.

Now silence. You can smell the gunfire. Slowly, you rise

still holding your hands up.

"They will do the same to you," one of the gunmen says. "Or worse."

"Come with us if you want to live," says another one with a wink.

Stepping around and over the body of the muscle man, they all make their way out through the swinging door. You follow them and move quickly to keep up as they walk in formation down the hallway.

As you pass each intersecting corridor, another two or three black-clad, ski-mask-wearing mercenaries join in, growing a long, single-file line of assassins. By the time you and the mercenaries reach the end of the hallway and exit to the deck on of the ship, the group is now an army of over 20 and everyone is armed.

There on the deck are another two dozen black-clad, armed mercenaries standing in a circle surrounding all of the dinner guests, hogtied and gagged.

"It doesn't have to be like this," you hear someone plead. It's Doctor Wexler, on his knees and bloodied, near the railing of the port side. "Please," he says to the three mercenaries standing over him.

The Doctor notices you with some delight, catching the attention of one of his captors who then says something in Mandarin and suddenly two mercenaries forcibly walk you to the doctor. Someone kicks you in the back of the knee and then the other knee, dropping you to the deck.

"Ah yes," one of the mercenaries says, removing her balaclava. "What good is a doctor without a patient?"

"Please," the doctor says. "Don't."

"Don't?" she says. "These greedy, evil pigs. These foul predators. They *don't* deserve to live. But you two? I may spare your lives because I may have use for you."

"You're not going to get away with this," says the Doctor.

The woman laughs, surveying the scene. "Get away with this?" she asks. "That does not matter. What matters is that these pigs, these American scum suckers, your friends... the only thing that matters is that they die tonight. Right now." She turns to the group and speaking again in Mandarin gives her orders.

Immediately, four of the masked mercenaries pass off their weapons and approach the group of hogtied hostages. Bending down to grab Mark Zuckerberg, they drag him along the deck ignoring his muffled screams. Reaching the rail of the starboard side of the ship, the mercenaries lift Zuckerberg off the ground, up higher than the railing, and throw him overboard.

The other hostages, writhing on the deck, moan and groan through their gags.

"They say drowning is a terrible death," says the mercenary leader.

Then, the mercenaries who threw Zuckerberg overboard return to the hostage group and drag Priscilla Chan to the railing.

Are you just going to sit there and watch them kill these people? They may be billionaires but they don't deserve to die like this. Or maybe you're ok with that.

Try to save the billionaires, turn to page 140.
Let it happen, turn to page 153.

You hand Beau the gun.

"You fuckin' sheeple," the man says, and spits at you.

You walk away, and head up the stairs out of the basement. You make your way into the living room at the front of the house, but from there you don't know where to go. You're trembling, your whole body is shaking. Your rage has turned to guilt to shame to confusion.

Can violence defeat violence? Is there another way?

Suddenly, the front door of the house bursts open as a SWAT team crashes inside with guns drawn.

"Get on the ground! Get on the ground right now!"

You put your hands up and slowly kneel but they're on top of you immediately, pressing your face into the floor and zip tying your hands behind your back.

Gunshots ring out from the basement.

A moment passes as you lie hogtied on the floor trying to suss out what movements you can from the commotion.

"Who zipped this bastard?" one of the SWAT team says. "Cut him loose, no prisoners."

Someone cuts open your zip ties and rolls you over onto your back. Standing over you are two heavily armored SWAT team members. One aims his rifle at your chest and says, "Where we go one, we go all."

He fires.

You did not survive 2020.

THE END

There's no stopping now. You stay the course and aim for a small gap between two of the SUVs. As the van careens towards the blockade, you brace for impact.

But before the collision, the armed men open fire, blasting you and the van with hundreds of bullets, ripping your body apart, destroying the windshield, the grill, the engine. You're already dead when the van crashes into the parked SUVs blocking the gate.

You did not survive 2020.

THE END

"OK," you say, "I'll come with you."

Holding the Glock in one hand Musk grabs Grimes by the wrist and runs with her towards the door to the cabins. You follow, chasing behind them now inside the ship and down the long hallway.

Running through the hallway you feel like it will never end, almost as if you're just running on a treadmill as the same walls and doors and walls and doors whiz past you. No one speaks as you all run, bumping along the walls as the ship rocks from side to side, and the only sounds are that of the baby crying and the arrhythmic thumping of your feet on the carpeted floor.

But there's the end of the hallway! Out the door, the three of you emerge onto the deck at the stern of the ship. The storm has really picked up now and the ship is careening viciously.

"To the pod!" Musk yells above the storm as a giant wave crashes upon the deck.

At the stern of the ship is a large, bright orange evacuation life pod angled down towards the water. It looks like a submarine with a small, windowed protrusion.

Musk reaches the rear of the pod and turns the large metal handle to open the waterproof door. Another massive wave crashes upon the deck. Musk helps Grimes step down into the pod with the baby. "Let's go!" he screams at you.

You don't hesitate and climb down into the pod after Grimes. Inside it's bigger than you thought with safety seating like you'd see on a rollercoaster for about 15 people. Grimes is seated holding the crying baby and buckling her safety belt. You sit across from her and buckle your belt as well.

Musk climbs down and closes and latches the big metal door behind him with a clang. He positions himself in the captain's seat at the back of the pod and buckles his safety belt.

"Hang on!" Musk says, and launches the pod. Your stomach rises and your feet lift into the air as the pod falls from the back of the ship. The collision with the water jerks you in your seat whipping your head back and forth.

The pod rocks violently side to side and feels like it may even roll completely upside down. Then you hear a loud hum and suddenly the pod feels more stable, moving forward. Musk has turned on the engine and is steering the pod out to sea away from the ship.

The pod is moving ahead steadily, the hum of the engine is comforting, and you find yourself letting out a sigh of relief.

The baby is no longer crying as Grimes rocks him while singing softly.

Musk sets the pod on autopilot and moves to the front where he finds a black duffel bag. Opening it up he pulls out a couple of towels and hands one to Grimes and one to you. You dry off your face and hair.

"How is he?" Musk asks Grimes.

"He's ok now," Grimes says.

"How are you?" Musk asks Grimes.

"I'm ok," Grimes says, now drying her face and hair with the towel.

"How about that Ba Jiao Gui?" Musk asks, laughing.

Grimes laughs, saying, "You're crazy, man. You're mad."

"I may be mad," Musk says. "But I make you happy!"

Suddenly, you hear a loud explosion from a distance and the pod is jolted forward.

"What was that?" you ask, as the pod rocks and sways from the blast.

"There goes the mighty vessel that was The Plutocrat," Musk says. "May she rest peacefully at the bottom of the sea."

"And all those people on board?"

"Dead," Musk says. "Or undead, I'm not really sure."

"This is insane," you say.

"You'll be fine," Musk says. "We'll be picked up in the morning and be at the facility by lunch time. We get to start a new life! The world will think we all died on that ship and now we're free!" Musk is now holding a bottle of champagne that he pulled out of seemingly nowhere. He pops the cork and the frothy wine pours out of the bottle as he hands you and Grimes each a champagne flute. "You can be whoever you want to be," he says, pouring you some champagne. "And we can be who we truly are!"

You look up from your champagne at Musk but it's not

Elon Musk anymore. Or is it? He looks green, scaly. You watch as he morphs into a reptilian humanoid. "There's nothing to stop us now!" he says, still sounding like Musk but without speaking, as if the dialogue is only in your head. The reptilian humanoid pours himself a glass of champagne and extends his glass out to Grimes. "Cheers!" he says.

Grimes says, "Cheers," and they clink glasses. She looks at you and smirks, saying, "You didn't really think he was human did you?"

You look back at the reptilian humanoid who is laughing and laughing and laughing. Then he says, "You didn't really think she was human did you?"

And you look back at Grimes and she is now morphing to reveal her true form as a reptilian humanoid. She is laughing too, as you watch the baby morph to reptilian humanoid.

The laughter echoes off the metal shell walls of the pod as the vessel slowly chugs away from the burning, sinking remnants of The Plutocrat.

"Cheers," the reptilian humanoid Grimes says to you and raises her glass.

"Cheers." says the reptilian humanoid Elon Musk.

Holding your glass of champagne, you stare at them both in disbelief. They look at you awaiting your cheers. Musk's green tongue slithers between his lips.

As weird as this may be, you have indeed survived 2020, congratulations.

"Cheers?" you say, raising your glass.

"Cheers!" they reply.

THE END

There's no way you're going to be able to break out of here, may as well wait it out. Even if you got out of this room, you're still on a yacht somewhere in the middle of the ocean, where you gonna go?

Suddenly, you hear gunfire. Lots of gunfire! An explosion rocks the boat back and forth. What the hell is going on?

You're at the door now trying to listen. But it's quiet. Wait, you hear something, someone talking, two people whispering, it's not English though, Russian? Yeah, maybe Russian?

You knock gently on the door. The Russian speaking stops. You knock gently again.

Slowly, someone opens the door. Standing before you are two large men dressed all in black holding machine guns. One of them speaks to you in Russian, maybe it's a question?

"Hello," you say. "My name is–"

The Russisans fire, unloading dozens of bullets that rip your torso apart and you're dead before your body hits the floor.

You did not survive 2020.

THE END

No one deserves to be murdered like this. You can't just watch this happen.

"Stop this right now!" you say.

All the mercenaries stare at you with their ski-mask eyes.

Suddenly Doctor Wexler leg sweeps one of the mercenaries who falls to the ground. The Doctor grabs his gun and before anyone can even react he's now holding the leader from behind at gunpoint. The mercenaries all point their guns at him.

"Nobody do anything stupid!" the Doctor says.

For a moment, the air is still and no one moves.

And then the Doctor's head explodes and his body crumples to the deck. It was a headshot from one of the mercenaries on the opposite side of the deck still holding his rifle aimed in your direction.

The leader looks at you and half of her face is covered in the Doctor's blood. Then she looks back at the mercenaries who await her order.

"This one too," she says. "But no mess."

Four of the mercenaries walk towards you.

"Wait," you say. "I didn't know he was going–"

But it's too late. The mercenaries grab you and fight as you might you're no match for their strength or numbers. Lifting you high into the air, they throw you overboard.

Hitting the water feels like hitting solid ground. You're completely disorientated, unsure which end is up or down and then you find the surface and gasp for air. The water is so cold it hurts.

You tread water as best you can in the undulating ocean.

The ship steadily travels away from you. What was once a massive vessel is now smaller and smaller and smaller as it sails into the distance.

On the horizon, you can see the pale blue light of dawn as your muscles seize and cramp and you succumb to the deep.

You did not survive 2020.

THE END

No one deserves what's happening to these people. You can't just leave them.

You run back inside and head straight for the control station and quickly study the grid of buttons, each grid delineated and numbered: Room 1, Room 2, Room 3. Within each "Room" are buttons for mic/speakers, clear/opaque, and open/close. But which room is which?

One of the humans is banging on the glass, but it only resonates as a soft, dull thud. You can see him talking, begging, but cannot hear his words. The girl is still cowering in the corner.

In the other room you see the reptilian humanoid, its face pressed against the glass, its torso rising and falling with its breath.

"This is room two," the creature tells you telepathically. "They are in room one."

You stare at the creature looking for any sign of malice, but you can read nothing.

"Open both rooms," the creature tells you. "Together, we will escape."

Can you trust this creature when it says the humans are in room one? Or is it trying to trick you into opening its room?

If it's telling the truth, the humans are in room one, but if it's lying the humans are in room two.

Hell, maybe you hould you open both rooms?

Open Room 1, turn to page 143.
Open Room 2, turn to page 146.
Open both rooms, turn to page 155.

You slam on the breaks. The van skids to a halt, rocking forwards and backwards from the momentum as you stare through the windshield at the bright headlights of the SUVs blocking the exit.

Through the blinding lights you can make out the armed men aiming rifles at you from behind the open doors of the SUVs.

A moment passes.

You shift the van into reverse. There must be another way out.

Suddenly, the men open fire, killing you almost instantly, and continue shooting into the van causing your bloodied body to bounce and shake like a ragdoll as the van crumples and dances under the attack of hundreds of bullets.

Within the hour, your body and the van are dumped into the East River and the next day the news reports on the continued nightly disturbances of fireworks throughout Brooklyn and the Navy Yard.

You did not survive 2020.

Your body is never discovered.

THE END

You press the open button for room one and watch as the door to the humans' cell opens. They come running out and don't stop. They run right past you and out of the laboratory.

"Wait!" you yell, chasing after them.

You catch up with them on the loading dock where you find them standing with their hands up, simple silhouettes backlit from the headlights of half a dozen large, black SUVs. A number of armed men aim rifles in your direction from behind the open doors of the SUVs.

You freeze on the loading dock alongside them.

One of the armed men in the darkness speaks through a megaphone: "Where is the creature?"

"It's still inside!" says the man. "We just–"

Suddenly, a hailstorm of bullets rip through the three of you on the loading dock. Hundreds of bullets shred and pulverize your bodies. You're dead before your bost hits the ground.

You did not survive 2020.

THE END

You run.

You run past the van as fast as you can towards the far entrance/exit that you clocked on the map when planning this action. Pausing in the nook of a building, taking a moment to observe the scene, you ditch your all-white jumpsuit, unzipping and stepping out, which leaves you in your black t-shirt and shorts.

Sticking close to the shadows and the building edges, you make your way to the unmanned turnstile exit, and you're out.

You jog across Flushing Avenue up Cumberland Street to the bicycle you locked up earlier. You unlock the bike, hop on, and ride up Cumberland, then left on Park underneath the Brooklyn Queens Expressway, then right on Vanderbilt… riding fast. It's late and you're the only one on the road and you make it to your destination: the corner of Vanderbilt and Greene.

Elliot Sutherland lives at 96 Greene and there it is, a simple brownstone. You dismount the bike and drop it on the sidewalk. Through the building's small gate, up the steps of the stoop to the front door, you catch your breath at the buzzer. You press the button for 3F, buzzing Sutherland's apartment, at first a few short bursts but then you lay on it like an unending car horn in gridlock traffic. Even from outside you can hear the buzzer inside his apartment three stories up.

You hear a window open and looking up you see Elliot's head looking down at you from the third floor. Releasing the buzzer, you step back from the building a bit to make sure he can see you. "Elliot," you whisper. "It's me. We need to talk."

"What?" Elliot says. "What the hell are you doing here?"

"Please," you say. "Can I come in."

Elliot darts back into his apartment. The window closes.

A moment passes.

The door is buzzed open, you enter quickly and quietly head up the stairs to the third floor where you find the door that reads 3F slightly ajar and step inside.

There's Elliot standing barefoot in sweatpants and a t-shirt in his kitchen. His arms are crossed and his black horn-rimmed glasses are slightly askew. Save for his longer, bushy hair, he looks the same as you remember him.

"What the fuck are you doing here?" he says.

"I have something you need to see," you say, handing him one of the GoPro cameras.

"What is it?"

"Please," you say.

Elliot snatches the camera from you and walks to his living room area: a nice couch, coffee table covered with books, green plants. He sits on the couch where his laptop is and sets up on the coffee table. He leaves the room and returns with a cord and connects the camera to his laptop.

You watch him watch the video. He stares intently at the screen and doesn't speak, doesn't move, doesn't even look at you for the duration of the video.

"That's you," he finally says.

"That's me," you say.

"Who else knows you're here?" he asks.

"No one," you say.

"WHO ELSE KNOWS YOUR HERE?" he screams.

You're stunned, shocked. "No one," you whisper.

"You need to leave right now," he says.

"What?"

"Leave," he says, sternly. "Right now."

"But I thought you'd be able to take this to the press, write a story, expose the truth."

"Expose the truth?" he asks. "Do you have any idea what you're dealing with? You've sentenced us both to death! Get out! Get out! GET OUT!"

Try to persuade him otherwise, turn to page 149.
Leave, screw him anyway, turn to page 151.

You press the open button for room two and watch as the door to the reptilian humanoid's cell opens. Slowly, the creature walks out and stands towering before you.

"Those humans are infected," the creature communicates telepathically to you. "We must kill them. Open the door."

"What?" you say. "No, we're not killing them."

The creature smashes it's large, clawed hand down upon the control panel triggering the door of the human's cell to open.

"Shoot the guards coming down the hallway," the reptilian humanoid tells you as he walks slowly towards the humans in their cell.

Somehow you know it is true, armed men are coming, and you quickly grab the other guard's pistol, crouch, and take aim at the hallway, firing as soon as you see the three guards running your way. You kill them all.

The reptilian humanoid is now inside the human's room, splattered in blood as it shreds and rips apart the female captive with its large claws. You can see the remnants of the man's body in a gooey pile in the corner of the room. Letting the woman's body fall to the ground in tatters, the reptilian humanoid walks back towards you now covered in blood.

"This way," it tells you.

Continue, turn to page 158.

The rain is coming down harder and waves are splashing up onto the deck. A lightning bolt streaks across the sky.

While it seems like either way you're screwed, there's something just not right with Elon Musk. He's desperate and panicked while Ba Jiao Gui and her awesome army of ninjas are calm and confident.

Besides, you feel like you should be on the side of the woman who disemboweled and strangled Jeff Bezos with his own intestines, no?

"I'm staying," you say.

A thunderclap reverberates through the air.

"Don't be stupid!" Musk says.

"Whatever it is you're up to," you say. "I don't want any part of it!"

"The choice has been made," says Ba Jiao Gui.

"Fine!" Musk says. "Stay here and die, we're leaving!" Grabbing Grimes by the wrist he runs with her into the cabin of the ship and out of sight.

Now, the black-clad army maneuvers to form a large circle on the deck. You follow along and join the circle with Ba Jiao Gui in the center. She speaks to the group in Mandarin Chinese. And you understand nothing. She continues, speaking louder, more forcibly, delivering an impassioned speech. And she finishes with what sounds like a question.

"Shì!" the group replies in unison.

Ba Jiao Gui asks another question.

"Shì!" the group again replies in unison.

Ba Jiao Gui asks another question, this time looking at you.

Everyone looks at you.

"Shì?" you say.

"Shì!" the group again replies in unison and all proceed to kneel. You also kneel.

Suddenly, Ba Jiao Gui begins to levitate, rising high above the deck. She outstretches her arms and looks up with eyes closed. Her appearance shimmers like a blue flame and it seems as though the sheets of rain are now passing through her as she ascends into the sky.

A woman from her army stands and walks to the center

of the circle underneath Ba Jiao Gui.

Lightening splinters across the sky and thunderclap rattles your insides.

You watch the woman standing in the center of the circle remove her shirt jacket to reveal some kind of homemade explosive strapped to her abdomen.

"Shì," chants the group. "Shì, shì, shì…"

Ba Jiao Gui begins to glow as this strange inner blue flame grows to engulf her while she rises higher and higher. "Shì, shì, shì…" the group chants.

Suddenly, Ba Jiao Gui lets out an ethereal scream that sounds something like a cross between a hurricane and a ship that's run aground… it's the last thing you hear before the explosives detonate, obliterating the yacht.

But those of you onboard, those loyal to Ba Jiao Gui, you are given the gift of eternal life. Or perhaps eternal damnation?

You join her as a member of her undead army, obedient and ever-serving, forever traversing the planet to convene, collaborate, and collect from the greedy and the covetous.

You did not survive 2020, and you will spend eternity in the service of Ba Jian Gui.

THE END

"Please!" you say. "I need your help. Those people died for this!"

"And so will we," Elliot says, foisting the camera and cord upon you.

"No!" you say. "No, we can get this out there, we can make this known!"

"Make what known?" Elliot says. "You think people are ready to believe this? To believe in green lizard men and mad scientists or whatever this is? Are you out of your mind? The world is just not ready."

"What are you talking about?"

"Look," Elliot says, now calming down a bit perhaps. "I've seen how these people operate," he says, sitting and putting on his shoes. "It's not as simple as you think it is. We need to leave."

Elliot heads into his bedroom and you can hear him rustling through his closet. "How did you get here?" he asks from the other room.

"I biked," you say.

"We'll take the train to Metro North," he says. "I have a place we can stay."

"But the subway isn't running at night anymore," you say.

"Shit," Elliott says, returning to the living room. "That's right." He's now dressed in all black, carrying a small duffle bag, and texting on his phone. He looks up at you. "You should change your clothes." Then he looks back at his phone.

It's the middle of the night. Who is he texting?

"I don't need to borrow any clothes," you say. "Where are we going? Shouldn't we upload the video? Make a copy?"

"Yes," he says, looking up from his phone. "That's a great idea. We'll download it so we have another hard copy." He sits back down on the couch with his laptop. "Give me the camera."

"I can do it," you tell him.

"Great," he says, standing and walking to the open kitchen.

You sit on the couch with the computer and plug in the camera but also quietly watch Elliot pace about the kitchen with his phone in his hand. After a few more minutes he receives a text perhaps, looks down at his phone, and then at you.

"Who are you texting?" you ask.

"What?" he says. "No one."

Then, Elliot steps to the apartment door and opens it to reveal two older men in black suits standing in the hallway. They step inside and close the door behind them.

"I'm sorry," Elliot says to you. "I didn't have a choice." Suddenly a blood-red circle the size of a quarter appears on his forehead and he drops dead to the ground.

One of the men stands there with his outstretched hand holding a smoking gun with a silencer aimed at where Eliot was standing. He then turns and aims the gun at you.

You click "send."

In the few minutes you just had while Elliot paced about, you uploaded the video to the cloud and included the link in a drafted email to every email address in Eliot's contacts including all his New York TImes and Los Angeles Times email contacts, and a few others.

The man with the gun stares at you with cold, unflinching eyes and pulls the trigger shooting you in the forehead right where you sit on the couch with the laptop on your lap.

You may not have survived 2020, but you and the others did not die in vain. The truth will be known, and the people will awaken.

THE END

"Fine!" you say, and grab the GoPro and the cable, and let yourself out, slamming the apartment door behind you.

You'll do it yourself. Somehow, you'll get this in the press and let the whole world know what's really going on. You won't let Quinn and Amos and Jonas die in vain.

You head down the apartment building stairs, out the door, down the steps of the stoop, and pick up your bike off the sidewalk. You walk the bike across the road to the other side of the street and mount the bike while passing underneath a large beautiful tree.

Suddenly, two black sedans drive up and park in front of Elliott's apartment. You duck down to hide in the shadows behind the tree and watch as one man from each car steps out and together they quickly trot up the stoop and somehow open the door and enter the building. Each car's driver sits motionless in their respective cars.

You watch, waiting.

In the silence of the night you can hear what you think is Elliot arguing up in his apartment? Is that him?

Suddenly, you hear a loud crash and look up to see Elliot falling from his apartment window landing headfirst on the sidewalk smashing his head open like a watermelon.

You cover your mouth to keep from screaming as tears roll down your face. You feel like you're going to vomit. And everything in your body says run but somehow you remain still and motionless.

The two men exit the building and walk around Elliot's body to return to their respective cars, climb in, and drive away.

Terrified to go home, you stay out all night and watch the sunrise from Ft. Greene Park where you stay until just before 10am when you walk four blocks to the Apple store on Flatbush. You're the first one to arrive when it opens and you pretend like you're interested in a new laptop and work with iMovie, which seems to convince the staff to let you browse freely.

Wasting no time you quickly make a new Gmail account and upload the video clip to a Google Drive folder. Then, you meticulously research, copy, and paste into the BCC field of an email all the contact email addresses of major news organizations including The New York Times, The Washington Post, The Los Angeles Times, and TMZ. You click send.

"You won't get away with this," someone says.

You look up and find an Apple employee talking to you.

"Wha– What?" you ask.

"You need any help with this?" the employee says.

"Oh," you say. "No, I'm just browsing, I'll have to think about it and come back." You grab the GoPro and walk quickly for the door.

Outside, the sky is bright blue and you can feel the warmth of the morning sun on your face. There's now a line of masked people waiting to enter the Apple store and the traffic on Flatbush crawls along with percussive horn blasts.

Who knows what comes next. If the press will publish these videos, if you'll be able to return to your normal life, if things will get worse before they get better… but for now, right now, you are here.

For now, you are alive, breathing, feeling the warmth of the sun on your face.

For now, you have survived 2020.

Congratulations.

THE END

Why risk your neck to save these billionaires. They'd probably just throw you in the ocean too!

"Please stop!" the Doctor screams. "No more!"

One of the mercenaries hits the Doctor with the butt of his machine gun and he drops to the deck. He's out cold, unconscious.

The mercenaries lift Priscilla Chan and throw her overboard. Then they return to the group and drag Warren Buffett to the railing. Another, bigger mercenary joins to assist the lift and they throw Buffett overboard. Then his three adult children, one by one, are thrown overboard.

Then the mercenaries toss Jeff Bezos and Lauren Sanchez overboard. Bill Gates goes next. Then Melinda and their children Rory, Phoebe, and Jennifer. Bernard Arnault and his five adult children are thrown overboard. Larry Ellison, Nikita Kahn, and their children Megan and David are tossed overboard. Next the mercenaries drag, lift, and throw Amancio Ortega, Rosalia Mera, and their three children. Then it's the Waltons that get tossed. And finally, the mercenaries lift in unionison and toss Grimes and Elon Musk overboard.

No one is left.

The mercenary army of dozens stands across the deck basking in their power. You remain kneeling next to the unconscious Doctor Wexler.

"Today," says the mercenary leader, squatting down to bring her face close to yours. "Today, we've made the world a better place."

"You murdered them," you say.

"Yes," she says. Then, louder, so all can hear her, she says, "And I may just spare you. I haven't decided yet!"

The army laughs, as if ordered to do so.

"In 10 days we will be back to Shanghai," she announces. "And with these American pigs dead and gone, no one will stop our nation from dominating this planet!"

"You won't get away with this!" you yell.

She turns to look at you and once again squats down to speak closely to you. "Do you like jokes?" she asks.

"What?"

"Jokes!" she says. "Do you like to hear jokes? I have a funny joke for you. It goes like this: As long as you may live, among the street rats in Shanghai begging for food... as many people as you tell this story to, rats and beggers and emassaries and police, no one, not one single person, will ever, ever believe you..."

With her face just an inch from yours, she cackles. "No one!" she says, and you can feel the spittle on your cheeks.

Standing again, she orders her army to commence their duties.

"That's not much of a joke," you say.

She glares down at you and smirks. "Not to you it isn't," she says.

The sun rises over the ocean.

Congratulations, you survived 2020 for, at the very least, one more day.

THE END

Screw it, let's go! You smash both open buttons and simultaneously both doors open.

The humans come out excited at first but then see that the reptilian humanoid's door is also open. "No!" the man screams. "No! No! No! No!" He grabs the girl and steps in front of her. "You let it out!"

The reptilian humanoid walks slowly out from its cell ignoring you as it moves towards the humans now retreating into their cell. The reptilian humanoid follows and attacks.

In swift, animalistic movements, the reptilian humanoid lunges first at the man grappling with him, lifting him off his feet, and slamming him to the ground. It then pounces on top of the man and viciously claws at his neck, digging into his throat, clawing away, nearly severing his head until the woman catches his attention.

She makes a dash for the door but the reptilian humanoid is quicker and leaps onto her back taking her down. Now prone, the woman scrambles and tries to crawl away but the reptilian humanoid gains control and repeatedly slams her face against the floor until her head is nothing more than a bloody pulp and bits of eggshell skull.

You smash the door close buttons, locking the reptilian humanoid inside the now bloodied studio cell. You watch as it stands to look at you through the glass. Its chest is covered in blood. Its hands are dripping blood. It stares at you.

"They were infected," it tells you telepathically. "They could not have been allowed to live."

"You murdered them!" you scream.

"They would've killed you and many, many others."

So many dead, so much blood: Amos, Jonas, Quinn, the two security guards, and now these two captives… you can't deal, this is too much.

"Let me help you," the reptilian humanoid communicates to you. "I can help you."

"Stop it!" you yell. "Get out of my head!"

"You must remain calm," it says. "You must trust me."

"You killed them!"

"And you will also die if you leave here without me."

Suddenly, you have a vision, something like a daydream, of you driving a car as a storm of bullets rip through the car and your body. It's just an instant but it feels so real.

"Trust me," the reptilian humanoid communicates to you. "Let me out or that will be your end."

Can you trust this alien killer?

Release the reptilian humanoid, turn to page 157.
No way, get out of there, turn to page 160.

You smash the button on the console opening the door to the reptilian humanoid's room.

It walks up to you and once it's within arms reach you cower but it does not strike you.

"Come with me," it tells you. "And you will be rewarded."

Continue, turn to page 158.

You follow it out of the laboratory, down the loading dock, and past the van, towards the river?

"Where are we going?" you ask, looking over your shoulder anxious there will be more armed guards.

The creature does not answer you and continues on its unhurried walk towards the water. Then, close to the edge of the old shipping docks of the Navy Yard, the reptilian humanoid stops. Together, you stand there looking out at the shimmering water of the East River and the glimmering city skyline of Manhattan in the distance.

In the sky you see a glint of gold, certainly not a star or the familiar flashing light of an airplane. Then you see another, and another. And now the lights are growing larger, some breaking into two or three separate lights, and you realize they're not only growing larger but also moving closer. As these lights descend from the sky you can now make out round or oval shapes surrounding the lights.

A fleet, a squadron of UFOs, alien spacecraft descend upon the city. One of the crafts descends towards you. Silently, with a soft blue light emanating from its underbelly and an occasional sparkle of golden light from its rounded sides, it comes down and stops maybe fifty feet away from you hovering just ten feet above the surface of the river.

"For millennia we have lived among you," the reptilian humanoid tells you telepathically. "Peacefully. Coexisting. Sharing with your species when needed."

Suddenly a cylindrical, bright blue light from the spacecraft shines upon you and the creature like a spotlight.

"But now," the reptilian humanoid communicates. "Now, the time of humans has come to pass."

Suddenly you feel weightless. And you can't breathe. There's no air! The blue light grows brighter and blinding.

Your feet touch down again and you open your eyes to see that you're now inside the spacecraft. The reptilian humanoid stands beside you and in front of you are a dozen or more other reptilian humanoids.

"You will be spared," the reptilian humanoid communicates. "With a select few others. But now... now is the time to end this scourge..."

You are now a witness to the violence and annihilation. Aboard the craft, you observe the devastating weaponry these creatures unleash upon the planet from their various ships.

The destruction spans the globe with such speed and brutal ferocity that news hardly reaches some pockets of civilization before they're destroyed. So much is destroyed in just minutes.

The world's armies are annihilated, many before having a chance to be deployed.

The attack is swift and merciless, sparing almost no one.

It's gruesome.

You are one of the very few who survive the reptilian humanoids' vengeful attack.

And this is just the beginning of the new world...

THE END

There's no way you're trusting this creature.

You run out of the laboratory, jump off the loading dock, and quickly climb into the parked van.

The keys are in the ignition and you start the engine.

You may not know much, but you know this much… it's time to go!

Continue, turn to page 130.

With merely a thought, you decline the offer.

The alien silently returns to the shadows and everything goes black. It's over.

You awake lying on your rooftop while the sun also rises behind the large UFOs hovering over Manhattan. As you get to your feet, you can't help but cough, loud and wet. Your head is throbbing with pain. You feel nauseous.

You stand there overlooking the city and think about the meeting with the alien. Was that real? Was it a dream?

You cough more, harder. Your hands are clammy. Do you have a fever?

As dawn greets New York City and the world enters a new chapter of cohabitation with extraterrestrials, you gaze out at the silver, stagnant UFOs.

Coughing, you have survived 2020... for now.

THE END

CAN YOU SURVIVE 2020

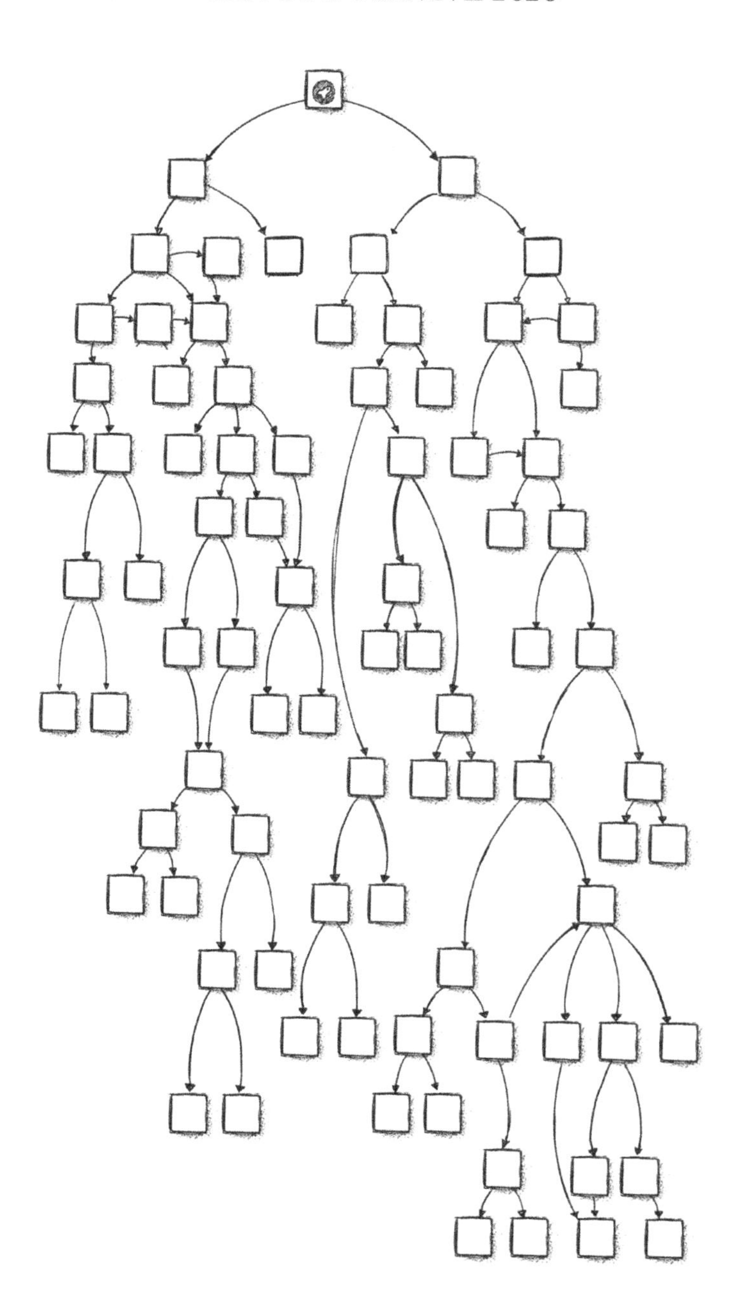

Andy P. Smith is a Brooklyn-based writer with published stories in Quartz, Vice, COLORS, and The Village Voice.

He is the author of the books *Welcome to the Land of Cannibalistic Horses* and *100 Things Phish Fans Should Know & Do Before They Die*. In his newsletter, THE MELT, he reports on climate change and our Anthropocene epoch.

An avid music lover and former impresario, Andy hosts a weekly freeform radio show.

You can find him on Twitter and Instagram at @apsmithnyc

Made in the USA
Coppell, TX
14 December 2020